BOUND TO THE BETRAYED

SUBMITTING TO MY STEPBROTHER
BOOK NINE

M. FRANCIS HASTINGS

CONTENTS

1

THE DEAL

Nate

Tracy Franz, as I live and breathe. She was the image of her mother. Beach blonde hair. Ocean blue eyes. As a transplant from California, Lillian Franz-Alton-Alejandro-FuckOnlyKnows had taken her strong genetics with her. There wasn't a lick of Morgan Franz in her.

It pissed me off. Everything connected to that woman pissed me off.

Especially the buxom, blue-eyed, blonde-haired replica standing before me, somehow with the gall to ask me for my help.

"What do you mean, you're in trouble?" I asked, as though I gave a fuck.

I didn't.

"Well..." She launched into an explanation, but I didn't hear a word of it.

All I saw were the perfect pink lips her whore of a mother lied to me through. Why should I have listened to more lies?

As her explanation went on, however, I shifted my attention and listened a little.

"... and Mr. Masterson is dead. And Gwendolyn is dead. And all these people are dead. And McKenzie's back on the run. And Will's been arrested for stuff his grandfather did. And they want to arrest me, too, for stuff my dad did. And if they do arrest me, I know I'm going to get killed in prison or something. I'm so worried about Will—he's my brother, you know? It's a really long story but my mother was his surrogate so, I guess technically, I'm related to the Mastersons. Which is a very, very bad thing. I'm going to get killed if you don't help me. I didn't know where else to go. You're the most honest person I know besides Will, and McKenzie and her family." She took a shaking breath. "And Gwendolyn."

I snorted. "Did you kill some innocent children while you were drunk behind the wheel or something?"

Tracy blinked at me. "Haven't you been listening?"

"Not to one word." I rose from behind my desk and leaned on the edge of it, folding my arms with a smirk. "You need a good lawyer, don't you? Is that the deal?"

"No!" she shouted, losing her patience with me. "I need an act of God!"

"Then why not ask your mother?" I inquired, quirking an eyebrow at her. "Obviously your father is fed up with you."

Her lovely chest heaved. "He left without me. I betrayed him, after all."

"Figures. You must have spent a lot of his money. But then, that's what you Franz women do," I said caustically.

She folded her arms over her chest so that we were mirroring each other. It was a shame. I'd had a nice view a moment ago. "I can't go to my mother," she continued, "because she is currently going through every rich man in Europe."

I chuckled. That sounded very much like Lillian. "I don't suppose you have any heartbroken swains of your own you can throw yourself on the mercy of."

"I wouldn't ask Bran Lockwood for a ride on a dark road with a serial killer on the loose," she said flatly.

"Oh, Bran Lockwood. We are making our way through the rich and famous." I expected to watch her squirm, but Tracy Franz, for all her failings, still had her pride. And I'd obviously reached the limit of what she was willing to take.

"You know what? You can go to hell. I thought you'd at least hear me out, but obviously I remembered you wrong. I'm just going to wander downstairs so I can be arrested or killed in front of your building. Wouldn't want to put it off any longer." She spun on her heel and, back stiff as a board, she headed for my office door.

I pressed a button on my desk and remotely locked the door. It might have been a performance—in fact, I was mostly convinced that it was—but the way her hand trembled on the door handle told me she was at least really and truly afraid of something.

She gave the handle a pull, but the door didn't open. She did it again, then turned and scowled at me. "Let me out."

"No."

"Why not?" she asked exasperatedly.

"It's hard to get bloodstains off the pavement," I quipped.

Tracy didn't find it funny at all. In fact, she paled a bit.

"I'm joking," I said, relenting just a bit. Playing with her was becoming more tedious than fun. I also wasn't immune to the fact that something was seriously wrong. Maybe if I'd been listening, I'd have been able to pick out the truth from the lies. Maybe.

"It's not funny," Tracy replied.

I wondered if she'd had occasion to see blood on pavement. My stomach tightened at the idea. She'd been a cute, care-free, young sixteen-year-old when I'd married her mother and had swanned over my estate the few times she'd visited, chattering nonsense with Lillian, and blissfully happy in the security money could buy. Though she and her mother seemed like two peas in a pod, Tracy was now not only older—twenty-four, now?—but also somehow more... jaded? She struck me as a person who'd seen some things.

Maybe she had seen blood on the pavement, and a body to go with it.

"All right," I murmured. "It's not funny."

"Look, Nate," she said, dropping all the polite civilities. "You're either going to help me, or you're not. By now, at least someone knows I'm here. This is where it's going to end for me. Either I get help, or I don't."

"Hm." I looked her up and down. What could I believe? Why should I stick my neck out for her?

And what in the nine hells had she done?!

I wondered if she was being dramatic, but she seemed to have been stripped of the capability of drama. Or smiling. The latter made me a bit sad.

"Well?" she prompted. "Help? No help? I've kind of got a deadline. Emphasis on dead."

She was being dramatic. I snorted. "And I'm supposed to help you just out of the kindness of my heart?"

"I was kind of hoping so, yes. You used to have a very kind heart," she said.

"Ah. Flattery. Flattery will get you absolutely nowhere with me. Your mother taught me that," I responded with a touch of bitterness. It had not been my intention to show emotion, but apparently I still wasn't immune to how Lillian had burned me. Especially when her spitting image was standing right in front of me.

"I am not my mother," she enunciated, clearly and coldly.

Maybe Lillian had burned a few bridges, if Tracy was unwilling or unable to go to her for help. Still, I couldn't help wanting my pound of flesh, and I knew exactly how to get it.

"I tell you what. I'll help you in whatever way you need if you sleep with me."

Tracy stared at me, incredulous. "Pardon?"

"There's those good manners from finishing school." I grinned at her. "It's a simple transaction. We go to that sofa right there and you give me what you've given out freely to every man who's winked at you since you were a teen."

She gave me a slight, very enigmatic smile. "You do think I'm like my mother."

I nodded. "And I figure I'm owed something for my help."

"Fine. Let's do it." She began stripping off her clothes. Her shirt and skirt hit the floor and she toed off her ballet flats.

Her bra strained to contain her breasts and her matching white lace panties made my mouth water. "All right," I agreed, making eye contact with her breasts. "Let's do it. But don't take off any more. I want to do that." I shrugged out of my jacket and took off my tie, tossing them on the desktop. My shirt followed after I carefully undid the buttons and cufflinks. I didn't want her to see me fumbling with anything. If she could be cool as a cucumber, then so could I.

I caught her staring at my chest and decided all the years of working out like a madman were utterly worth the trouble. Of course, I'd begun putting more effort in after Lillian left me for that damn actor. But it was worth it just to see the look on Tracy's face.

"Don't worry, babe. It's about to be all yours," I murmured, gripping my belt and pulling it off. I toed off my loafers before dropping my pants.

Then she was staring at the front of my black silk boxers, where I was already sporting a semi. "That's yours, too."

She swallowed. "Okay."

My socks went next and then I walked over to her, stalking her as though she were prey. "Do you like it hard or soft?" I asked, brushing her beautiful wavy, blonde hair over her shoulder.

"Uh… whatever you want." She'd lost some of her bravado, but I chalked that up to desire. I was a catch. She knew it. I knew it. And she was a catch, too.

"I'm glad you understand the rules of the game," I said, sliding my hand down to cup one of her luscious breasts through her bra. Her nipple hardened under my palm and she gasped, her pupils dilating.

I flicked her nipple with my thumb and she gave a very satisfying moan. Her body was so responsive. I couldn't wait to be inside it.

I unhooked her bra and she let it slide down her arms, revealing perfect pink nipples. "God, you're beautiful."

"Thanks?" she replied, sounding uncertain.

Considering she'd been with Bran Lockwood, and he was an ass, I decided she probably hadn't gotten a lot of compliments recently. That was a crying shame. "You are," I assured her and pressed my lips to hers.

Tracy immediately opened her mouth to receive my tongue, stroking hers tantalizingly against mine.

I pulled her hips flush against mine, letting her feel my hard cock. She drew in a sharp breath, her arms winding around my neck, her luscious breasts rubbing against my chest.

"Have you ever had an older man?" I asked, raising my head and backing her toward the couch.

"You're not that old. You're only fifty," she scoffed.

"True. But have you?" I tipped her back on the leather sofa and followed her down so she was laying beneath me. I didn't bother asking about a condom. She would definitely be on birth control, given her recreational activities.

"No," she admitted. "But if you have me now, that will change."

"You're damned right it will." I slipped off my boxers and then her panties, teasing my fingers into her blonde curls. She was so wet it made my dick twitch. "I think I'll have you a few times–I want to get my money's worth."

She shrugged. "Whatever you want, Nate."

"That's right: Whatever I want." I lined myself up. "And right now, I want to screw your brains out, Tracy." I shoved my cock into her, hard and fast...

... And ran into something completely unexpected.

But it was too late by then. She arched her back and cried out in pain, not pleasure.

"Shit," I swore. "Shit. Fuck. Shit." I froze above her, not entirely sure what to do.

"Will you... please... just finish..." she requested, her voice shaking. She'd closed her eyes and hidden them with her arm, her pride clearly not allowing her to let me see her cry.

Even if I'd wanted to, I couldn't continue. My dick was just as disgusted with me as I was and by the time I pulled out, he was no longer 'happy.' "Jesus Christ, Tracy, why didn't you tell me?!"

"Would you have believed me?" she asked softly.

No. I would have laughed in her face. We both knew it. I looked down and saw a smattering of blood on Tracy's thighs, evidence of what I'd just taken from her.

Looking down at myself, I saw her blood as well. I wanted to be sick. I got up and strode over to my desk, grabbing my jacket and letting everything else fall on the floor. I tossed the jacket over her, then pulled on my boxers and sat in the chair next to the couch.

"Okay," I said quietly. "I'm sorry. And I'm listening."

2

MERCY

Tracy

Something about his words made me burst into hysterical laughter. "Sorry," I giggled. "It's all been a little much—"

The intercom on Nate's phone buzzed. "Shit," he swore. "Who the hell wants me at this hour?"

"It's the FBI," I said, still laughing as I dropped my head into my hands. "God, this is surreal."

He got up and crossed to the desk, stabbing a button. "What?" he snapped over the intercom.

"Sir..." I recognized the voice of the guard who'd shown me upstairs. "The FBI is here."

"The..." He looked at me, then at the desk phone, then back again. "Tell them to wait."

"They're not willing to wait. They say they have a search warrant," the security guard replied.

Nate glowered at the phone. "For what? And on what grounds?!"

"For Tracy Franz. They say their surveillance team saw her coming into the building—"

"And you saw her leave an hour ago," Nate said forcefully.

The security guard didn't miss a beat. "I did, sir."

"So, they can just be on their way."

"Mr. Alton, this is Agent Jared Perth. I'm afraid we're going to need to search the premises. Tracy Franz is a wanted criminal and needs to be brought to justice," came a new voice.

"Do you have a warrant? We have proprietary information here. I can't just let you all traipse through the building," Nate seethed.

Perth continued as though he hadn't been interrupted. "We have a warrant."

"Great, I dispute it. You'll be hearing from my lawyer very shortly. You might as well wait in the lobby," Nate said smoothly.

"Until that time," Perth persisted. "We have the right to conduct a search. Starting with your office."

Nate looked at me. "My office?" he growled. "You think I'm letting a bunch of FBI agents comb through *my* office?!"

"I do, sir. We're not going into your computers. We're just searching areas where she could be hiding." Perth paused. "You know harboring a fugitive is a federal crime."

"I'm aware," Nate said icily. "Which is why I'm not. Like I said, I sent her on her way. I don't know, maybe she called an Uber. Check with them."

"Good. We will. But first, we're just going to verify that what you're saying is true." The line went dead.

Nate swore. He started gathering up my clothes.

"Are you turning me in?" I asked, getting up from the sofa.

"What? No. It would take a fuckload more than that to get me to turn you over to them," he said. He thrust my clothes at me. "Get dressed."

I pulled on my clothes quickly while Nate donned his. Once my left shoe was on, I heard the nearby ding of the elevator.

"Damn it." He led me behind his desk.

"I think they're going to find me pretty quickly if I hide underneath," I pointed out.

"I know." He opened a small cabinet.

I stared. "You expect me to fit in there?"

"It's deeper than it looks." He reached in and slid back a panel that was obviously meant to hold a safe but was currently empty. "Get in."

I still wasn't sure I was going to fit, but with few other options, crawled backward into the cabinet and crouched down. He slid the secret panel back over me, leaving what I was sure was an empty cabinet above.

Or not, I reflected as something clattered above me. Maybe he was filling it up?

I heard, and felt, the cabinet door close with a small reverberating snap. There was a louder banging a short distance off and I imagined it was his large, wooden office door.

"Come in," he said testily.

"Mr. Alton," I heard Perth say. "Thank you for seeing us on such short notice."

"Just do your fucking search and leave. My lawyers are tearing apart your warrant as we speak," Nate replied. "You're not going to get any further than this office."

"We'll see," Perth said.

I wasn't sure what silent cues he used, but the FBI's feet fanned out around the office and a bunch of loud rifling commenced.

"Sir, could you please come out from behind your desk," Perth asked.

"No. I don't think I could. Why, you think she's underneath?" Nate scoffed.

I could feel Perth losing patience in the tartness of his next words. "Please, Mr. Alton. Don't make me remove you."

"Another complaint to add to the dispute," Nate said. But, he stood and walked past the cabinet where I hid to get out of Perth's way. Then I realized the cheeky bastard *sat* on it.

While I was sure Perth was examining the empty space under Nate's desk, I struggled not to break into hysterical laughter again. It was all so surreal.

A phone rang. I heard Nate answer. "Richard, I texted you twenty minutes ago! There are fucking FBI agents in my office with a fucking warrant. Can you please dispute the warrant before they tear apart the whole building?!"

I didn't hear Richard's response, but whatever it was pissed off Nate. "I don't want to hear your excuses. I don't care if you're at a wedding being officiated by the Pope himself. Get your ass on it!"

Feet thumped around the floor. There wasn't one corner of the office that was left unsearched as far as I could hear.

"Mr. Alton, please move," Perth said suddenly. "I'd like to check that cabinet."

Nate snorted. "A five-year-old couldn't fit in there."

"Nevertheless, I'm going to check it," Perth insisted.

I could almost hear Nate rolling his eyes. There was a creak of him standing up, then shuffling aside. "Be my guest."

Swallowing, I heard the cabinet door open.

Then shut again.

"I suppose we'll just have to start checking the rest of the building," Perth said.

A different ringtone sounded. "Yes?" Perth answered. Then he growled. "It's a legitimate warrant, Grant. You know that and I know that. What, does he have a judge in his pocket or something?"

"It's been good to see you. Truly the highlight of my day," Nate snarked without waiting to hear any more. "Now get out of my building."

Perth didn't move. I couldn't see them, but I imagined them locked in a staring contest, waiting for the other to flinch. Even crammed into the little hiding space I was in, I could feel the tension.

"Well?" Nate snapped.

With great reluctance, Perth's footsteps began thumping on the floor. "This isn't over, Alton," he sneered.

"Pretty sure it is, but you hang onto that little shred of hope you've got there. And call Uber." Nate leaned against my cabinet.

Other shoes began shuffling out of the office. Soon, the heavy office door closed with a loud slam.

Nate waited.

I waited.

He pushed off the cabinet and crossed to where I knew his desk to be. "Adam?"

Adam replied over speakerphone. I recognized his voice. It was the security guard who'd been confronted by the FBI. "Mr. Alton?"

"Are they gone?" Nate asked.

"Yes, sir. Agent Perth was calling Uber on the way out."

"Good. Keep up the good work." Nate ended the call and his footsteps returned to the cabinet.

In short order, whatever items he'd put on top of me were chucked out and the panel was drawn back. He gripped me under the shoulders and helped me get out.

I should have expected it, but it slipped my mind that spending so much time rolled in a tight ball was going to have an effect on my muscles. As soon as I was standing, I swayed against him, gripping his shirt for balance.

His strong arms wrapped around me, and when I looked up, his face was inches from mine. He stared at me. I stared back.

I licked my lips out of reflex and he followed the movement. Then he took a deep breath. "You need to be careful."

"Careful?" I echoed. For some reason my heart was pounding.

"Your legs probably fell asleep while you were in there," he continued.

I'd been thinking of a different kind of 'careful' but he was absolutely right. "Yes, of course."

He regarded me another moment, then swept me up in his arms as though I weighed nothing. I gasped, quickly putting my arms around his neck to steady myself.

Nate walked over to the sofa and gently deposited me on the cushions. "Just sit here a while and wait for the pins and needles to go away."

I nodded.

He settled himself in an armchair opposite me. "Let's start over. Tracy, what the *hell* is going on?!"

"So much. I don't even know where to start," I responded, dropping my head into my hands.

"The beginning," he demanded, but kindly. "Start at the beginning."

So, I did; at least *my* beginning. I told him about how I'd come into contact with McKenzie and Will, then formed a bond with them through Gwendolyn. Then subsequently learned of Masterson's corrupt organization and that my own father was deeply involved in it.

"To make matters even weirder," I sighed. "It turns out Will Masterson the Third is my half-brother. My mother donated an egg back in the day and... well... that was that. Now, we're all in trouble with the law even though all we did was try to take down the whole Masterson ring. McKenzie escaped, but they got Will. I've got a target on my back, too. They weren't lying when they said if they go down, they're taking us with them."

"And you couldn't go to your father or mother for help?" He said it more as a statement than a question.

I grimaced. "My dad has disowned me. He fled and basically told me I'm on my own. And, well–you know Mom. She doesn't want to screw up her new relationship by having me around."

"Of course," he snorted.

"I couldn't think of anyone else to turn to, honestly," I said softly. "You're the only truly good person I know in our circle. Or, I guess, who's ever *been* in our circle. I wouldn't insult you by suggesting you're still dragging yourself through the mud with us."

Nate gave me a tight smile. "'Good'? Like how I took advantage of you not two hours ago?"

"Er... well..." I winced. "Okay, not one of your finer moments, but..."

"I'll help you." He nodded sharply. "I've got a house in Ecuador. I'll tell my pilot to get the jet ready and we'll go down there."

"'We'?" I asked, confused.

"I'll get you settled, then fly back here and start the necessary investigations and legal proceedings to clear your name. It's a nice house, but it's rather remote, so I just want to make sure everything is prepared for you. There is a housekeeper I usually use when I'm there, but I don't go often so I want to make sure she is available," he said.

I really hadn't expected him to go so far for me. I'd thought he might throw some money my way, but this was beyond anything I could have hoped for. "I don't have my passport," I suddenly realized.

"You wouldn't be able to use your own passport anyway," he replied. "We'll have to have a fake one made for you."

"Do you know people who can do that?" I asked, feeling suddenly cautious.

Nate chuckled. "I'm not a saint, Tracy. I know people who know people. I can't say I've had need of their services yet, but we're in a bind. Hopefully they can expedite the process, whatever it is, and have some documents made for you within the next few hours. I don't trust Perth as far as I can throw him. They're staking out the building, I'm certain of it."

I felt sick. "Not surprising, I guess."

He slid off his chair and came to the sofa, sitting down next to me. "I'm going to take care of you, Tracy. It's going to be okay."

God, I hoped he was right.

3

THE DOCTOR IS IN

Nate

Mr. Sneed looked and sounded like a Dr. Seuss character. His hair was right out of Whoville. His quietly correcting voice reminded me of the Lorax. And he had enough stripes of varying widths and colors running through his clothing to rival the Cat in the Hat. But, my contacts assured me he was *the* best, and fastest, forger in the Midwest.

Sheer politeness stopped me from asking how he kept attention off himself in his getup. I just hoped he hadn't alerted Perth, wandering around looking like a truffula tree.

"I was reading *Oh, the Places You'll Go!* at a library for some kids," Mr. Sneed said suddenly. "I don't usually bring that into my professional life, but hey. You said it was an emergency and you transferred me enough money that I wasn't going to drive forty-five minutes the other direction just to change clothes. I didn't want to waste any of your precious time."

"Ah. Yes." I wondered where this impromptu explanation was coming from.

"You were staring. Well, glowering, really," Mr. Sneed explained.

I was beginning to wonder if the man was psychic. "Apologies. It's just that, unfortunately, I think the FBI are watching this building. I was afraid you might draw... unwanted attention."

Mr. Sneed shrugged. "At this time of night? I could have rappelled down the side of the building in a catsuit and slipped in through a window and still have drawn attention. Trust me, they clocked me the second the guards let me into the underground parking garage." He raised an eyebrow at me. "You know, I've stayed under the radar for years. I'd never take a job like this if the money weren't tremendous."

"If the FBI ends up giving you any trouble, the money will go from 'tremendous' to 'unbelievable,' I assure you. I don't believe in interfering in a man's livelihood," I said.

He smirked. "Says the business tycoon. Aren't sales and acquisitions kind of your thing? Putting people out of jobs?"

I narrowed my eyes on him. "That's not the way *I* do business."

"Uh-huh. Okay, off with that one, on with the brown one," he said to Tracy.

She pulled a red wig off her head, breaking her stillness now that the camera was off her–and her silence. "Nate? Exactly how much is 'tremendous'?" she asked me softly, while Mr. Sneed looked over the photos he had thus far.

I squeezed her shoulder gently. "Never you mind."

Tracy didn't like that response. I could see it in the way the corners of her delectable lips tightened, the narrowing of her eyes, the impertinent upward tilt of her chin. But, most endearingly, the mutinous scrunch of her nose. Her mother had never done anything like that. Especially not when she was getting what she wanted. "Nate—"

Unable to help myself, I booped the tip of her nose. She might not have had the red-haired wig on anymore, but I knew I was playing with fire. "Nate!"

"Hush. What's happening now is what needs to happen. You don't need to worry about it. I have lots of money. I like giving it away to worthy causes. I consider you a worthy cause," I said.

She stared at me for a moment. Her eyes began to well up with tears and she quickly turned her face away.

My heart, which I'd thought I'd buried under an avalanche of bitterness, constricted. I touched her hair. "Tracy, you are more than worthy. You have to know that. If your mother and father haven't been telling you that…" Morgan Franz had abandoned her and Lillian had rejected her. She'd told me herself. Why would two people that selfish have ever told their daughter she was

worthy?

Tracy looked up at me with the saddest smile and in that moment, I would have given my entire fortune to cheer her up. "Really? You went there?"

I grimaced. "Yes, well, I momentarily lost my head and forgot your parents aren't worth the paper their pictures in the tabloids are printed on." I dropped my hand, feeling awkward. "I just… wish things had gone better for you, that's all."

"Me too."

"Brown! You're supposed to be in the brown wig!" Mr. Sneed barked.

I hastily stood back while she scrambled for the mannequin head with the brown wig on it. She smiled for real now, though, so I decided an extra hundred-thousand to Mr. Sneed wouldn't go amiss.

In the end, it took around four hours to get Tracy set up with proper fake IDs. While waiting, I arranged an expensive (yet necessary) show for Agent Perth. I just hoped Tracy was too preoccupied with Mr. Sneed to know just how many zeros were being tacked onto her escape to Central America. I knew she wouldn't like it.

"Now, once you get where you're going—don't tell me where— you want to keep one of these IDs on her person; two accessible at all times, and one hidden in a safe place," Mr. Sneed instructed me, handing me Tracy's IDs.

"Thank you," I said. "We'll do our best for Tracy not to have to burn through these."

"Well, if you do, just call me. That extra hundred-thousand was much appreciated," he replied quietly.

Though, it seemed, Tracy still managed to hear. "Extra hundred-thousand?" she murmured to me as he gathered his things and left my office. "How much did he cost before that?!"

"Don't worry about it," I said absently. "Now, I believe new clothes and some luggage have been delivered. Why don't you pick out what you like and go pack?"

"Nate, if you don't tell me what things cost, how am I going to pay you back?" she sighed.

Pay me back? I stared at her. "Tracy... your father ran off with your fortune. Your mother has turned you away. And your parents thought the best use of your mind was to send you to finishing school. Unless your goal is to one day marry into money, at this time, it seems unlikely you will *ever* be able to pay me back. You... understand that, right?"

She blinked at me. Then her eyes widened as though realization had hit her right between them and she stumbled backward to sit heavily on the sofa. "Oh."

I went to her side, inexplicably drawn there. I sat on the coffee table across from her and took her hands in mine. "It's all right. Breathe."

"It's not all right!" She looked glum. "I really want to be able to pay you back. You don't owe this to me, Nate..."

"No. But I want to help—and I'm going to. That's the end of it," I said firmly.

Tracy swallowed. "If this is about the sort-of, almost sex..."

I winced. "No. I mean, I can't say that isn't part of it, but no. I feel guilty, but not guilty enough to do all of this." I squeezed her hands. "Just let me do this, all right? We'll go down to Ecuador, get you settled, and I'll work on things on this end. I think all of you in this situation are going to need very, very good lawyers. I can't imagine that Will doesn't already have one, but I am going to look into it. No one—*no one*—should ever have to suffer like this for doing the right thing."

She looked up at me and gave a little laugh. "You sound very patriotic right now."

I squared my shoulders. "A man has to stand for something."

"Don't take this the wrong way," she said, lowering her eyes. "But you're very handsome when you're crusading. Just an observation."

My heart pounded. Hell, I still wanted her. I turned my crusader inward to hunt down the dirty old man who was having such thoughts. I also gently released her hands. "We need to get you packed."

"Right." She started to rise, but I shot up quickly so I could help her, even though she didn't need it. The smile she gave me made the awkward gesture completely worth it.

I escorted her to a conference room, which was lit up with the windows tinted to full obscurity. Five racks of clothing in her size were lined up in front of them.

Tracy went to one of the racks and pulled off a ski suit. "Um... this is for Ecuador?"

"No. I just told my shopper that they should grab a variety of things for destinations unknown. Can't give the FBI any clues, now can we?" I responded, leaning against the wall as I watched her browse.

She laid things out on the conference table, then pulled over a set of Louis Vuitton bags and began hastily packing.

"We're not in a rush. The jet will wait until we're ready to go," I reassured her.

"Yes, but I'm taking up so much of your time!" she fretted. "And I know the longer people have to wait, the more you have to pay them."

"*Please* stop worrying about the money." I sounded sharp without meaning to, but in truth, I was getting a little annoyed. I wanted it settled between us.

Tracy's shoulders drooped and I felt like an ass. In her shoes, my pride would be screaming.

I went over to her and took a sarong from her frozen hands, laying it back on the table. "I'm sorry," I said softly. My hands chaffed her upper arms. "I'm sorry. I know this is all a shit situation for you. I'm—"

She walked forward and buried her face in my shoulder.

Reflexively, my arms closed around her and hugged her against me as she began to cry. "I'm sorry," she choked. "I'm just... it's just... I don't mean to fall apart on you..."

I stroked her hair. It was so silky. I lamented the idea of her putting it up under a wig. "Listen, Tracy. You are the bravest person I've ever had the privilege of being in the same room with. You're not falling apart. You've just had a very rough day."

Tracy gave a wet chuckle. "I guess I have."

I gave her a squeeze, then released her. "Feel better?"

She nodded, her cheeks flushed.

I didn't want to read too much into those red cheeks. They were probably pink with anger at her situation or embarrassment over breaking down in front of me. Any other options were not acceptable.

"I think I can finish packing now," she said softly, after a long silence.

"You do that." I perched myself at the other end of the conference table and pretended not to watch her as she packed and pretended I couldn't see her folding the lovely undergarments that had been ordered for her. I really did try my best to look away at that point, but my mind conjured even more lurid images of lingerie sliding silkily over her skin as I dragged it off her body.

I tried to remember I was the white knight in this scenario. A white knight who had already done something truly unforgivable. If I had a prayer of retaining my status, my white knight—my crusader—was going to have to hunt my inner dirty-old-man much more diligently. Where did I get off lusting over a twenty-something who was young enough to be my daughter, anyway?

For the longest time, I'd wondered what my colleagues were doing–throwing away lives, marriages, children, whole fortunes–on women whose only redeeming attributes were regularly injected with filler. It made no sense. Sure, any red-blooded man could agree that younger women were beautiful. But at our age, I figured we should be well past thinking with our dicks. I'd even counseled a few of them about it, which didn't make me the life of the party, but it did give me a certain smug satisfaction of having the moral high ground.

Now, here I was, lusting after Tracy. I could just hear my friends now, laughing their asses off.

"Do you have a particular problem with this nightie?" Her voice broke through my thoughts.

I blinked, seeing the black piece of lingerie for the first time. "Shit."

She turned it around on the hanger. "Is there a hole in it?"

Given all the lace and see-through material at the bust, there might as well have been. "No, it's… it's fine. I was thinking of something else."

Tracy smiled. "I thought so. I was just teasing you."

Her smile made my heart pound in my ears.

I was so fucked.

4

ON A JET PLANE

Tracy

Nate was not just smart, he was positively diabolical. I'd been wondering how we were going to get out of the building without the FBI chasing us.

Ten—*ten*—limousines showed up to the building as we made our way to the underground parking garage. I only knew because Nate kept confirming their arrivals with security. He'd also hired actors to dress up like me and take those limos off on wild goose chases all over the city and even into the suburbs.

"It's too much. Seriously, don't you have to pay all those people?" I asked as the parking attendant handed him a set of keys.

"Never you mind," he said again, wheeling two carry-ons behind him and hefting another three bags. All of them are mine.

I, rather guiltily, lugged a small purse and medium-sized bag of personal items. I really shouldn't have packed as much as I did, but since I was going to be tucked away in Ecuador for the foreseeable future…

"Are you sure you don't want me to carry something else?" I asked sheepishly, knowing I wasn't going to get anywhere with the conversation about how much my escape was costing him.

"No. I want you to follow me, get in the car, and be safe," he grunted.

I didn't remember Nate ever being this infuriating, but then he'd been my mother's husband and not mine, and–as usual–I'd tried not to get too involved. Certainly not attached. I just felt bad that Nate was the only person who didn't know my mother would eject him from her life as soon as she found something "better," in her estimation.

With a sigh, I gave in. I was in Nate's capable hands, and I was going to stop questioning my good fortune. It was certainly worth a little discomfort and the loss of my virginity, as underwhelming as that had been. To me, the trade still seemed terribly one-sided.

"We're here." He stopped next to a nondescript, tan sedan that was perhaps three models old. He pressed a button on the fob and the trunk opened.

"Should I get in?" I asked.

Nate turned to look at me. "I haven't unlocked the car yet, Tracy."

"Oh… no… I meant the trunk," I stammered.

"What? No. That shouldn't be necessary. You've got your wig on. I'm just going to load up the luggage." He lifted the bags into the trunk. At least, those that would fit. He still ended up putting one of my bags, plus the one I was carrying, in the back of the car.

I winced. "I should have packed lighter."

He shook his head. "Better to be overprepared. The house is rather remote, and the less activity going to and from it, the less chance there will be of you being discovered. Ecuador doesn't have to extradite you, but they have that right."

My stomach knotted. "I hadn't thought of that. I sort of thought once we got there, I'd be safe until everything got worked out."

Nate paused and put a hand on my shoulder. "That's the idea. I just want you to be cautious. I don't think anything will happen, honestly. I think you will just have a nice, long, restful vacation until everything can be sorted out."

"Okay." I still couldn't shake the sick feeling in my stomach. I was about to go to a foreign country, in the middle of nowhere, to *hope-*

fully lay low for God-only-knows how long. Alone. "This could take years, couldn't it?"

"Yes." He didn't look happy about his response, but I respected the fact that he didn't lie to me.

"Okay," I said again. My heart sank, but I kept that to myself. I hated being alone. And for that amount of time? I was sure to go crazy.

Apparently my face wasn't onboard with keeping my feelings to myself, however. "I'm going to get the best lawyers for all of you, Tracy. Hopefully, things will be resolved quickly," he encouraged.

"Sorry. I'm not trying to be ungrateful. And… thank you. You're really… I just can't begin to…" My throat choked up and I couldn't get the rest out.

He wrapped me in a hug that made me feel safe. "It's okay. You don't have to say anything."

"But you're doing so much!" I managed.

Nate gently rubbed my back, calming me down. "It's the right thing to do. You all have suffered too much."

I looked up into his brown eyes, which had gone warm like melted chocolate. There was something more than sympathy there, but for the life of me I couldn't figure out what it was. It made me feel melty, though and I could feel my cheeks heat up.

He released me quickly. "Anyway, we should get going."

"Right. Yes." I slid into the passenger seat.

Nate got behind the wheel and started the car, putting it in gear. He took a deep breath. "Here goes nothing."

Then we drove out of the parking garage.

I hunched my shoulders as we passed cars parked along both sides of the street, wondering which might be the FBI.

"Don't hunch over. It makes you look suspicious," he instructed me.

I straightened up quickly. "Sorry."

"Nothing to be sorry about. It's not like you make a habit of going on the lam." His small smile was infectious and I gave a nervous one in return.

"Don't turn around, either. I'll keep track of whether or not we're being followed," he said.

"Okay." My neck cramped with the effort of not letting curiosity get the better of me. I stared straight ahead and watched him flick his eyes to the rearview mirror as he drove.

Finally, Nate turned fully-around, quickly, to glance behind us as we exited onto the highway. "I think we foxed them."

"That's great!" I replied with a nervous smile. A thought occurred to me and my tentatively relieved mood went up in a puff of smoke. "Do you think they're staking out the airport?"

"They're welcome to. I sent the jet somewhere else," he said with a cat-who-got-the-cream grin.

I blinked. "Are we meeting it on an empty stretch of highway or something?"

"No. There's a small airport in Rochester. Very small. But it suits our purposes just fine."

That actually made a lot of sense. The Mayo was in Rochester. It would be a good idea to have an airport for those coming from around the world to seek treatment.

Another thought occurred. "But… won't they flag your jet?"

"It's not my jet. I called in a favor from an old acquaintance," he said. "As long as the pilot knows his way to Ecuador, we'll be fine."

I couldn't think of any other obstacles. He had flawlessly handled everything. Relief washed over me and I sagged bonelessly in my seat.

He put a gentle hand on my knee. "I promised I'd make it okay, and I will. Trust me."

"You're the only person I can trust," I admitted softly.

Nate squeezed my knee, then returned his hand to the steering wheel. "We'll be there in a little over an hour. Why don't you get some sleep? You've got to be completely wrung out."

"I'm afraid if I close my eyes, this will all be a dream and I'll be in FBI custody with my brother," I said.

He glanced over at me. "I'm here. Nothing's going to happen to you."

"I know. But my nightmares don't," I mumbled.

Nate paused, then offered me his hand. "Would it help if I hold your hand while you sleep?"

I swallowed and slipped my hand into his. "I think so."

He smiled and my breath caught. "Good."

I hurriedly closed my eyes, but it was too late to stop me from feeling all gooey inside. What was I thinking?!

Nate just calmly held my hand in his warm one. It was also slightly rough, not smooth like most in our social circle. He did, or had done at one time, some manual labor.

Sleeping was out of the question now, of course, but I didn't tell him that. I just kept my eyes closed and soaked in the warmth of his hand. I listened to him breathe and the slip of his other hand along the leather steering wheel as he drove. Surprisingly, or perhaps not-so-surprisingly, these things were more calming to me than any amount of sleep–or so I thought.

My wig was askew when I woke up. That was my first realization. I must have rubbed it on the seatback because more of it was in my face than on my head. My hand was also cold. His hand was gone– and so was he.

I panicked. "Nate?"

My door opened and I jumped, just barely stifling a shriek.

"Shh," Nate murmured. "Come here. I'm just going to take you to the jet."

"Take me?" I asked, blinking sleep away.

Then he scooped me up in his arms, careful not to knock my head on the doorframe.

I automatically put my arms around his neck. "But... I can walk..."

"Not today. You were sleeping so soundly, I hoped I wouldn't wake you. You just rest on me," he said.

Honestly, I was too tired to argue. I let Nate carry me onto a small jet and deposit me on a sofa. I looked at the back of the jet and saw our luggage already tucked into a nook.

I turned to him and experienced another gooey moment when he looked at me. Gooey turned to something more intense as his chocolate brown eyes smoldered. I might have been newly de-virginated, but I could still read that expression.

He still wanted me.

Though, I had a feeling he wasn't going to touch me again without a wide-open invitation–and maybe not even then.

Guilt flickered in his eyes and he looked away. "Go to sleep, Tracy."

As I thought. "I'd rather talk."

Nate looked back at me. "About what?"

God, how to even approach this subject? What am I doing, anyway? What do I actually want from him? My mind spun. "About... stuff." *Lame!*

"You want to talk about what happened between us back in my office," he surmised correctly.

I scooted over a little and patted the sofa next to me, finally remembering I'd been to a very nice finishing school. Girls from very nice finishing schools did not leave a man standing while they sat through (what I assumed would be) a rather lengthy conversation.

He glanced at the open spot. "I'm not sure that's a good idea, Tracy."

"What's not a good idea?" I asked.

"Sitting next to you."

"Why not?" Then, I was on the receiving end of another burning gaze. My throat went dry. I had to clamp my legs shut against a wave of desire.

"You know why not," he said, his words more of a growl than words.

My heart pounded in my ears. "It's okay."

Nate snorted. "You, my dear, like to play with fire."

"So I've been told," I admitted. I gave him the most stubborn look I had in my arsenal.

He stared me down. Neither of us budged.

Finally, he sighed and sank down next to me. I tried to hide a triumphant grin.

"Don't get too cocky. My old ass was just getting tired of standing. Plus—"

A smiling, middle-aged woman in a sharp skirt and matching blazer came through a set of curtains from the cockpit. "The captain says we'll be taking off now. Please remain seated until we've reached cruising altitude. The captain will let you know when you are free to move about the cabin."

"Thank you," I said politely. It was a good thing politeness had been drilled into me until it was second nature. My entire brain and body's focus was currently on the fact that Nate's thigh was flush against mine.

"You're welcome." The flight attendant then left us in peace, disappearing back behind the curtains.

This left us in silence with thighs touching, and the air heavy with lust.

5

UP IN THE AIR

Nate

She can't possibly want me after what I did to her, I tried to convince myself. Still, there we were, our legs rubbing against each other as the jet taxied and took off into the air. I burned where we touched and it was positively maddening!

Maybe this is her revenge, I mused, biting the inside of my cheek to try to stave off a raging erection. I could already feel I was losing. And I completely deserved whatever vengeance she decided to mete out.

The plane bucked suddenly and Tracy's perfectly manicured nails dug into my thigh. I swallowed a yelp and slid my hand into hers instead. "It's okay. I'm sure it's just—"

"Sorry, folks, it seems as though we hit some turbulence," the pilot laughed, right on cue.

Tracy squeezed my hand. "Right, of course." Still, she looked pale.

I transferred her hand to my other hand so I could put my arm around her. Our hands were now joined right in my lap–a new form of torture. "It's okay. The pilot knows what he's doing. No need to worry."

She leaned my head against my shoulder and let out a sigh of relief that made me feel like Superman. Yes, I was perfectly capable of protecting her. And I was going to. Because...

It's the right thing to do.

Even as I thought it, a devious little corner of my brain began laughing maniacally. *Fuck that. You're doing this completely because you want her. Your brain has left the building and your dick is now completely in charge.*

I swallowed. I tried to deny it. But there was at least a part of me, no matter how small, that wanted another chance at being between her legs, this time to make her cry out in ecstasy and not bite her tongue against pain.

The expression on her face haunted my memories. Which was why I newly resolved myself to a monastic life as long as I was with her. My dick could fall off for all I cared. Tracy did not deserve to be manhandled by me again.

"What are you thinking about?" she asked, rubbing a finger over my eyebrow.

That one small gesture was nearly enough to melt all my resolve. *I am so fucking screwed.* "You," I said without thinking.

Her bright smile lit me up from the inside out. "Really?"

I cleared my throat. "Well, yes. Have to get you settled and all that."

"Oh." She looked disappointed for the smallest of seconds, then brightened again. "I'm still so grateful, Nate. You have no idea."

She wanted to kiss me. Her gaze landed on my lips.

"Tracy," I said sternly.

Her eyes flicked to mine. "Yes?"

"No."

She looked confused. "No what?"

"No wanting things you shouldn't," I chastised her. Though, it was mostly a warning to myself.

Tracy paused. "Why not?"

"Because I'm old enough to be your father and I just did something unforgivable to you. I know you're grateful to me, and I can understand how that could be confusing..." I began.

She pressed her lips into a thin line. "I see."

"Good," I said, trying to feel relieved. But it just dissolved into disappointment. "Because—"

"I see you're an idiot." She crossed her arms over her ample chest.

"Pardon?" I replied.

Tracy stubbornly turned her face to the window, not answering me.

It was probably for the best. I settled back against the sofa and pulled out my phone, ignoring her as well.

At least, trying to.

Unsuccessfully.

Her warm perfume wafted over work that blurred on my phone and I squeezed my eyes closed, trying to clear my head just as much as my vision. I counted backwards from a hundred, trying to drown out the smell of her on the air and the feel of her against my thigh. I should have moved anywhere else on the plane. But my protective side wouldn't let me abandon her.

I got to 'one' and started back over at a hundred.

Sixty-five... sixty-four... I started forming the numbers silently with my lips.

She shifted and I lost count.

Ninety-nine... ninety-eight... ninety-seven...

"Is it because I remind you of my mother?"

My eyelids snapped open. "Because what?"

Tracy rolled her eyes at me. "You're not old enough to be deaf. I asked if you don't want me because I remind you of Lillian."

"Don't... want... you?" I sounded like a stuttering neanderthal, I could hear it myself, but the concept was just so outrageous that there wasn't any other way to say it. It was as though I was repeating a foreign language.

"Yes. You don't want me. I figured it out. I was just hoping it wasn't because of *her,*" she said.

My jaw was on the floor. I was less surprised when I was in a new high school and my fellow students tricked me into getting changed in the girls' locker room. "I don't want you," I repeated for clarity.

"No. You don't want me. I mean, I'm not an expert, but I think when you want a woman, it–you know–stays hard when you're doing it," she continued.

My manhood would have taken a hit back in the day, but I was older and wiser now, and she needed a little of that wisdom–before she ended up doing or saying something stupid later with the next man.

The next man. I growled.

She blinked at me. "Nate?"

Fuck it. I pulled her into my lap, gripping her ass as I crushed my lips to hers.

Tracy squealed in surprise, then fisted her hands in my shirt and moaned into my mouth.

I was hard. I'd been nearly there since the moment we sat down thigh-to-thigh. Now, with her in my lap, I was grinding on her like a school boy anticipating his first time. But then, so was she.

With great effort, I tore my lips from hers, which resulted in a sound of protest from her. I pressed my lips to her ear instead while pushing one hand up under her shirt and bra, getting a lovely handful of her perfect, plump breast. "Tracy," I whispered hotly.

"Uh… uh-huh?" She gasped as I thumbed her nipple.

"I don't give a *flying fuck* about your mother." And I meant it, for once. I had someone much better squirming in my lap. Everything about Tracy blasted Lillian right out of my mind and wounded heart, a feat no other woman had accomplished in all these years. And I'd only known her for a few hours!

She shivered, winding her arms around my neck. "Kiss me again?" she begged–as if she needed to ask. I dragged my lips back to hers.

Tracy was practically riding my dick and I had her shirt and bra pushed all the way up, feasting on her nipples, when a soft 'ahem' brought my brain out of its fog.

We weren't alone.

"I'm sorry, Mr. Alton. I was just wondering if either of you would like a beverage or something to eat," the flight attendant said.

I quickly pulled my jacket up around Tracy's shoulders, disappointed that I would not be initiating her into the mile-high club today. She wasn't some slut who wanted an audience. I could tell by the way she was blushing. "We're fine, thank you." I tried not to snap.

"It's a long flight. Are you sure?" the flight attendant pushed.

I looked at Tracy. "Do you want anything?"

Her blush deepened. "N-no."

That was an obvious lie. She wanted me cock-deep inside her just as much as I wanted to be there. But as far as food and beverage went… "We're both good, thank you."

"But—"

I narrowed my eyes at the flight attendant in the same way I did to my business colleagues when they were being difficult. "Is there a problem?"

"No! No problem," she said quickly and finally, blessedly, scurried away.

I turned back to Tracy and, with deep regret, smoothed my hand over her breast before popping her back into her bra and pulling her shirt down. "Sorry. I didn't mean for us to become exhibitionists."

She laughed, tapping her forehead to mine. "Maybe we can pick this back up when we get to Ecuador."

Her smile warmed me more than I wanted to admit, especially to myself. "I'd like that."

"Me too." She seemed reluctant to get off my lap. Hell, *I* was reluctant for her to get off my lap.

"Did you… um…?" she asked.

I grinned. "As much as I enjoyed our little session—no, no I didn't. And you didn't, either. So I guess we're both going to be frustrated for a while."

Tracy sighed and finally flopped back down onto the spot next to me. "Tell me about it."

Gently, I kissed her neck. I ran my fingertips down her arm. "You are exquisite, Tracy."

She shivered. "You're making it hard."

"You have no idea," I chuckled. Reluctantly, I stopped and settled for holding her hand. "I shouldn't be doing this, you know. I practically assaulted you earlier. You do remember that?"

"I do." She nodded. "But I'm not going to cut off my nose to spite my face."

"What do you mean by that?" I asked, confused.

Tracy turned slightly and took both of my hands in hers. "I think you were an asshole before. But you're not now. And I'm attracted to you, despite what happened. So, I guess I'm saying I'd be willing to forgive you for one really good orgasm." She grinned at me.

I squeezed her hands. "It's cute that you think you're getting just one," I murmured.

"Good. I'm glad you're on board. I—"

"Mr. Alton, are you sure you don't want a beverage?" The flight attendant was back.

I was going to have to put a bell on her–she was far too quiet. I glanced at her and tamped down on my rage. "No, thank you," I said firmly.

Though I expected her to leave, this time she didn't. She shifted from side to side in her low heels and began wringing her hands. "I really must insist—"

"'Insist'?" I echoed, frowning. "What do you mean, 'insist'?"

"What's her deal?" Tracy whispered to me.

I shook my head in bemusement. "I have no idea."

Tracy looked past me and gasped, her eyes going wide and terrified.

I whipped back around, only to find myself facing down the barrel of a gun.

"You should have chosen the beverage," the flight attendant said harshly.

I moved to block Tracy with my body. "What do you want?"

"My payment." She leveled the gun at my chest.

"Listen, I don't know who is paying you to do this, but I'm sure I can double their fee," I replied, casting about for something—anything—that would get us out of this mess.

"You probably could, but I have my reputation to think of. Night-night, Mr. Alton."

She shot me.

Tracy screamed.

I looked at the dart sticking out of my shoulder and realization dawned. "We're being kidnapped," I mumbled to Tracy as the drug began to kick in.

6

HOTEL CALIFORNIA

Tracy

Cool, callused fingertips trailed across my forehead, brushing the hair out of my eyes. I opened my eyes to see Nate leaning over me, his chiseled jaw stiff with concern.

"Are you all right?" he whispered.

I smiled at him, remembering his mischievous smirk all the other times I visited my mother. "I'm fine. Why so serious?"

His dark brown eyes narrowed and his hand moved down to squeeze my shoulder. "Tracy, where do you think we are?"

"Your mansion, of course. Where else would we be?" My head throbbed. My hand lifted to my forehead, only to encounter a bump and some dried and not-so-dried blood on some gauze. "Did I hit my head?"

"Yes, sweetheart, you did." He left the chair he was sitting on and lowered himself carefully beside me on the edge of the bed. Taking my hand, he said gruffly, "We need to get you to a hospital."

"I'm surprised Dr. Raymond isn't already here. He must have another emergency," I mused, thinking of the private doctor that served a good number of wealthy families in our area.

Nate took a deep breath. "How old are you, Tracy?"

I frowned. "What kind of a question is that? Eighteen." I turned my head, but my vision swam so I decided to give up on that. "Where's Mom? Plastered or primping?"

"Honestly, I don't know. We're... not together anymore, Tracy. And you're not eighteen. You're twenty-four." He spoke the words carefully, as though expecting me to have a bad reaction. He wasn't wrong.

"What?!" I shot up–then groaned, wanting desperately to throw up. A dented, metal, plastic-lined garbage bin appeared just in time.

When I was finished, he set the bin aside and helped me lay back down, cradling my head all the way down to the flat pillow. It smelled funny in here—like someone had tried and failed to take out the stale smell of years of cigarette smoke with dollar-store cleaner.

Nothing around me was familiar or made sense except Nate. When he drew his hand back and began to sit up, I gripped his arms, holding onto him with a desperation bordering on panic.

"It's all right, sweetheart. It's all right. I'm not going anywhere." He stopped in place, not pulling away.

"M-maybe we should go to that doctor now," I said, my voice shaky in my ears.

His eye ticked just where it crinkled up slightly at the corner. He was older than when I last saw him, now that I had a good look. I wondered what I looked like. I was afraid to find out. "About that..."

The door banged open and it was as though an explosion had gone off. I couldn't help it–I cried out in pain.

"Is she awake?" A woman I didn't recognize, but a niggling sense told me I should, stood in the doorway with her hands on her hips. There was an unconcealed shoulder-holster on her, boldly confronting us with its dark gun inside.

"As I told you before, she needs a doctor," Nate responded angrily. "She's had some sort of head trauma. She doesn't even know what year it is."

"Sounds like you're doctor enough for this situation. We don't need her to know the year. She just needs to be alive when the client comes," she sniffed.

"What?! No! I'm a businessman. I'm not any kind of doctor," he objected. "Don't people like you have nefarious underground doctors who show up when you call them? You must get into all sorts of situations. This could be life-threatening. There's no way for me to know."

The woman looked me up and down with scorn while my heart pounded, the words *life-threatening* echoing over and over in my head. Finally, she gave an exasperated sigh. "I suppose if we want her alive in two days, we're going to have to sink more into the operation than we wanted to. Damn. I hate paying for doctors." She shook her head and walked back out the door, slamming it behind her.

My head exploded with pain again.

"I'm sorry, sweetheart. She's a real bitch," Nate said, stroking my hair.

Slowly, I turned my head so my cheek was against his palm. "Have we been kidnapped?"

"Yes."

I appreciated that he didn't try to sugarcoat it. "Why?"

"You got mixed up in something and came to me for help. We were going to fly to Ecuador, and I was going to come back to clear your name and help your friends, who are also tangled up in this mess. I don't know the whole story. I know enough, but not all of it. You were trying to tell me, but…" He looked away, ashamed.

I touched his cheek, turning him back to face me. "But what?"

He swallowed hard. "But I wouldn't listen and abused you instead."

"Abused me? Abused me how?" I lightly tapped the gauze on my head. "Was this you? What did I do to make you mad?" Hurt settled in my heart. I'd always thought he was a good guy.

"What?!" he blurted, so loud it made my head throb. He noticed and lowered his tone. "No, you hit your head on the armrest of the jet, or so they tell me. I'd already been knocked out. I… well… I cornered you into agreeing to have sex with me in my office."

My nose crinkled. "Excuse me? Why would I even do that?! What about Mom?"

"Your mother and I haven't been together for nearly six years," he sighed. He hung his head in shame. "And you didn't do anything but come to me, when you had nowhere else to go. You did nothing wrong, Tracy, and even if you had, I still had no right to touch you. I wanted to punish her, not you."

"I swear, I'm going to start calling her Lillian. Who did she cheat on you with?" I grumbled.

"It doesn't matter. Probably more than one person. I didn't know who she really was when I married her," he said. "The point is that I took all those years of bitterness out on you. I thought since you look like her, you must be like her. I was stupid, insensitive…"

"You were a real bastard," I concluded for him.

Nate gave a self-deprecating smile. "I was."

"And you were trying to make it up to me by taking me to Ecuador," I guessed.

"Yes."

I scowled at him for a moment, thinking all of it over. "Well, was it good, at least?"

"What?" he asked.

"The sex." I gestured vaguely. "Was the sex any good?"

He winced.

"Well fuck," I muttered. "Not compatible or something?"

"Nothing like that. It was my fault. There was a problem that I couldn't get past," he told me.

"Problem? Oh! Right. At your age… I mean, that's natural and totally not a big deal," I said quickly, inadvertently glancing down his body.

Nate made a choking sound. "No. That part was perfectly functional, thank you very much."

"So, what went wrong? I mean, you're handsome and you haven't been married to my mother for six years. You're old enough to know your way around the block. What happened?" I asked.

"I was ready. You weren't. It… I… deflowered you," he responded, his features tight with shame.

A myriad of emotions washed over me, but the overpowering one was how ridiculous all of it was–from Nate "deflowering" me, to getting kidnapped. I didn't live that kind of life. I never had. I started laughing.

"Tracy?" His head came up and he searched my eyes. "Are you okay?"

"'Deflowered'? Really? What century do you live in? Oh my God, I can't believe I got to twenty-four years old without losing my virginity. Lillian must have been a real cautionary tale." I giggled. "I'll bet you pulled right out and we didn't even get to finish."

"Well... yes, that's true. But I should never have done it in the first place," he argued.

I kept laughing. "Ugh, a disappointing first time with a guy who should know better. I might as well have lost it in the back seat of a truck to a sweaty boy in high school."

He grimaced. "When you put it that way..."

I squeezed his arm. "Nate, don't worry about it. I still think you're a good guy."

"I don't. But that hasn't stopped me from lusting after you." Heat sparked in his eyes and I swallowed, feeling scorched from the top of my head to the tips of my toes.

"Had we... made an arrangement to take care of that?" I asked hoarsely.

Nate nodded. "Yes."

"When are we going to do it?" I moved my hand up to stroke his cheek, his rough stubble just fanning the flames.

He turned his head and kissed my palm. "I was going to have you once we got to my house in Ecuador, though we were having some trouble keeping our hands off each other in the meantime."

I grinned, feeling all tingly and gooey at his kiss at the same time. And that was just my hand! "I like that plan." Then, the fact that I'd lost six years of my life and had just been kidnapped slammed into the forefront of my mind, and my smile faded. My heart rate picked up and I started gasping for air.

"Hey. Stay with me, sweetheart," he said, gathering me against him. I felt his lips brush over my hair. "I said I'd take care of you, and I will."

I curled my fingers into his shirt, laying my ear over his heart and using its steady rhythm to calm my own. "Nate?"

He rubbed small circles on my back as my breathing evened out. "Yes, Tracy?"

"I'm glad I went to you for help. No matter what happens, I'm glad. Thank you for helping me." I wrapped my arms around his waist.

Nate looked down at me with molten chocolate eyes. "I'm going to make it all better. You'll see. Soon, we'll be making love on a big canopy bed in my house in Ecuador. And after I've cleared your name, we'll do it again in my penthouse. And my mansion. And every goddamn place you or I can possibly think of."

"Don't you think you'll get tired of me? I mean, we haven't even properly done it once yet," I reminded him with a laugh.

His voice went low and gravelly. "I already know I won't get tired of you."

"How?" I whispered, mesmerized as we locked eyes once more.

"I'm more than twice your age, sweetheart. I know a few things." He looked at my tingling lips, then lowered his head…

… and kissed my forehead.

I tried not to be disappointed, but my expression must have given it away, because he chuckled.

"Oh, Tracy. Let's get you healed up before we go any further. Twenty-four already makes me feel like I'm robbing the cradle, but eighteen-year-old you would be criminal," he said.

"Not according to the law." I tried not to sound petulant. I failed.

He gave me a heart-melting smile. "Perhaps not. But I do want you to be able to properly remember what happened in my office and make an informed choice."

"What was my choice when I was twenty-four?" I asked.

Nate cleared his throat. "You wanted it."

"Good. Sounds like me." I started to nod, but thought better of it. I didn't want to set my world spinning again.

"Tracy, sweetheart, there is nothing I'd like more than to pin you to this bed right now and fuck you until you can't walk," he said, and the crassness of it made me shiver. "But you need that head wound looked at and, honestly? I'd rather not have an audience barging in on us. There's that woman and the man who was our pilot. They were hired to procure us and they're giving us to someone else. I don't know who. I do know you need to be healthy for when we make a run for it."

This time I did nod, and regretted it instantly. "Ow."

As if on cue, the door opened.

Nate sat back in his chair as the woman from before entered with another woman in tow. I blinked as the second woman came into view. "Kinsley?"

7

BROTHERHOOD

Nate

I saw a dandelion poof of pink hair over goth or emo clothing. Honestly, I'd never known the difference and this did not feel like the moment to ask for an education.

"Well don't you look like you walked out of a biker shop!" Tracy laughed and I tensed.

"Tracy, I don't think we should insult the docto—"

"And you look like you walked into a wall," Kinsley replied with a grin, folding her tattooed arms, making her leather, studded vest creak.

Tracy pointed at the woman I'd come to know as Irena. "Arm rest. Ask her."

Irena scowled. "Can we get on with things, please? Dr. Farrington, the package has a head injury…"

"She thinks she's eighteen," I added before Irena could gloss over the fact.

"That's too bad, considering her ID's going to say she's twenty-four," Kinsley said, frowning herself.

"She doesn't have an ID. Not a real one, anyway," Irena sniffed. "Does it really matter?"

"Well, if it's a brain bleed and she dies, it's going to matter an awful lot to your client." Kinsley's tone was bland but her eyes were troubled.

My chest tightened. "You can't let her die." I sounded very authoritative, without any authority over the situation at all.

"I don't intend to." Kinsley turned to Irena. "We need to bring her to the warehouse. I'm going to need to give her a CT scan."

"What? Really?" Irena huffed.

Kinsley raised one pierced eyebrow. "She doesn't know what year it is. That's kind of a bad sign, don't you think?"

Irena threw up her hands. "Fine. Just, fine." She pulled out her cell phone and was soon yelling into it. "Jacques, we're going to the warehouse!"

Tracy winced and I stared death at Irena for hurting her.

"Tone it down, Cataracts Casanova," Irena snarked. "It's not like we did it on purpose."

"Thank you, lovely kidnapper. It warms my heart to hear you say so," I snarked back. It wasn't one of my finer moments, and certainly, as a man in my fifties, I should have risen above, but I wasn't feeling particularly mature in that moment.

Irena laughed. I wanted to punch her. "You're pretty spicy for a guy who needs a pacemaker and a bottle of Viagra to—"

"Are we planning to leave sometime today?" Kinsley sighed. She pointed at Irena. "You—get your colleague and get the car ready. You —" She pointed at me. "—how strong are you?"

"I don't have a pacemaker, if that's what you're wondering," I said.

Kinsley gestured to Tracy.

"What?" Tracy asked.

"Can he lift you?" Kinsley looked between the two of us.

"Pretty sure he already did," Tracy responded, glancing at me.

I stood and slid my arms under Tracy.

"Try to keep her as still as possible," Kinsley said. "We don't want to make her injury any worse."

"All right." I very carefully lifted Tracy in my arms and cradled her against my chest. She snuggled right in, laying her head on my shoulder. My heart thumped in my ears.

"Let's get her down to the car." Kinsley gave Irena a pointed look and the mercenary stomped over to open the door.

Jacques was outside, looking equally peeved. "Is this really necessary?"

"Yes," Kinsley said. "And the longer you stand here whining about it, the longer it's going to take."

He swore loudly in at least five languages, then he stormed down the stairs ahead of us.

I saw then that we were in a run-down motel. Not that I was surprised, given the condition of the room we'd been in. The air was also warm but dry. I decided we were still in the United States as I took in the restaurants and gas stations around us, and we definitely weren't in Minnesota–probably one of the more southern states. Beyond that, I had no clue.

"Well, are you coming?" Jacques demanded, pulling me from my guesswork.

"With bells on," I replied, carefully carrying Tracy across the parking lot. Irena and Kinsley followed behind.

Even if I could make a run for it—and I very much doubted I could with two mercenaries surrounding me—I didn't think jostling Tracy in her current state was a good plan. She needed help and it seemed this Kinsley person could provide it. I resolved to look for better opportunities in the future.

Jacques stopped beside a black SUV. I just barely managed not to snort.

"What?" he asked, frowning at me.

"I was just thinking how bad guys in movies always drive black SUVs–and here we are," I said.

He glowered at me. "Just get in the damn car."

It was on the tip of my tongue to say something snide, but that was the advantage of being a man in my fifties. I knew when to keep my damn mouth shut.

I gingerly slid into the back of the SUV when he opened the door.

Once I got us settled, I realized Tracy had fallen asleep. "Shit," I mumbled, looking around for Kinsley.

Jacques tried to get in the back seat next to us while Irena got behind the wheel. I blocked him with my arm. "We need the doctor. She's out cold again."

"For the love…" he grumbled. "She can take a look at her once we get to the warehouse."

Kinsley shoved him out of the way. "I need to see my patient. You can sit in the front."

"You can't just…!" He balked.

"Jacques, just get in front. I'm tired of this whole thing already and the longer you bitch about it in the parking lot, the longer this is going to take," Irena snapped.

He glared at me, at Kinsley, then grumbled under his breath as he went to the passenger seat. He slammed the door while Kinsley slid in next to Tracy and me. She took out a flashlight from one of the many pockets in her black, studded cargo pants and leaned over Tracy, pushing her eyelid up and flashing the light in her eye.

She did the same with the second and frowned as she clicked the flashlight off. "Definitely a CT scan."

"Uneven dilation?" I asked, trying to hold Tracy as still as I could while Irena peeled out of the parking lot and into traffic.

Kinsley nodded. "I don't even have to guess that it's a concussion. Now I just want to know where and how bad."

"And… are we going to the hospital?" I hazarded. "For the scan?"

"We're going to the warehouse," Irena said firmly. "Don't think you're wiggling your way out of this one!"

"She needs a CT scan!" I barked back. "You've got that in a fucking warehouse?!"

Kinsley patted my knee. "Don't worry. I've got everything at the warehouse." She was trying to reassure me, but I'd done enough business deals in my day to see the tight lips and shifting eyes. She was worried about Tracy.

This, of course, fanned my worry into a full-blown forest fire. I held Tracy just a little tighter. "You're worried," I murmured.

"I am," she whispered back. "But the warehouse really is a state-of-the-art facility. I wouldn't have it any other way."

"Hm." I tamped down on my panic. I needed to concentrate on what I could control in this situation that would help Tracy get better. This led me to glance speculatively into the front seat.

Kinsley shook her head vehemently. "Not now," she hissed. "After. I'll help you. But there is nothing you can do right now to make the situation any better. Just keep Tracy still until we get there."

'I'll help you?' I eyed her from her pink hair to her black, studded boots. "We'll see."

"What are you two yakking about back there?" Jacques asked angrily.

"How not to let half of your package die," Kinsley snapped back without missing a beat. "Can you drive any faster?"

D-I-E?!!! I tried to lock eyes to confirm what she'd just said, but she avoided mine. Which was a sort of confirmation. *Fuck!!!*

"You want us to add the time it will take to break free of a police chase?" Irena said.

"Not really," Kinsley replied.

"Then shut up and let me drive," Irena grunted. "We'll be there in fifteen minutes."

Fifteen minutes was not nearly soon enough in my opinion. "Are there any hospitals closer?"

Jaques turned around to look at me. "Mr. Alton, I know you're some kind of big shot in the huge metropolis of Minneapolis, but here–that don't mean shit. Now shut the fuck up."

"What my esteemed colleague means, Mr. Alton, is that no, there are no hospitals closer at this point, and even if there were, we wouldn't be going," Irena said, glancing in the rearview mirror.

If fate were to grant me one wish, it would be that, if Kinsley indeed did get us out, I would have my hands around Jacques's throat before we left. It had been a while since I'd seen the light go out in a man's eyes, but the violent, nasty spark in his needed to be extinguished. I knew that kind of light when I saw it. Some men just wanted to burn the world for fun.

I knew he saw the answering light in my own eyes and the slight upturn of the corner of his mouth said he accepted the challenge-welcomed it, even.

He and I had, by mutual agreement, just engaged in a very dangerous game.

"Jacques, no," Irena admonished him.

We broke eye contact. "What?" he asked.

"He's part of the package. You don't get to fuck around with him," Irena said firmly. "It's bad enough we'll have to explain Miss Franz."

He thrust his lower lip out in a petulant pout. "If she dies, there's no point, is there? Then can I have him?"

"The client still wants him. He was very clear," Irena insisted. "So, no."

"Damn it." He hunched in his seat.

While Jacques appeared to be a man in his mid-thirties, he was acting like a thirteen-year-old. I wondered if he was brain-damaged or if he just had a bad childhood. I was leaning toward the latter. Regardless, when the time came, I wasn't going to hesitate. It wasn't my job to psychoanalyze him. It was my job to put him down like the monster he was.

"It would be harder than you think. I'd recommend giving up on the idea," Irena said while he grumbled under his breath. Her eyes didn't leave the road, but I knew she was talking to me. "I can't say as I was able to get into all those classified military operations, Sergeant Alton, but I imagine whatever you did there has you all puffed up now, thinking you can turn this situation around. But now you're a man in your fifties, remember? That was all a lifetime ago. Hell, some of it happened before Miss Franz was even born. You really think you could measure up now against two trained, younger, professional mercenaries? No. You've been behind a desk far too long. I mean, it's all very admirable what you've done with your life, and how the military was able to provide you with a top-notch business education and all that. Scraping it all together and building up an empire from nothing? That's something, but it's not going to help you here. You can't buy your way out of this. You can't negotiate your way out of this.

Let's face facts, shall we? You're stuck. Best thing you can do for you and Miss Franz is not make trouble."

If she'd taken a different path, I could have imagined myself hiring Irena as head of my legal team. Pity. "I wouldn't dream of making trouble. As you say, my military career was a very long time ago," I responded. "Not that I did anything truly dangerous. I'm sure you saw in my file that I was in communications."

Irena cackled. "Yeah, right."

Yeah, right. I silently agreed.

8

COMING AROUND

Tracy

My head was throbbing like someone was knocking on my temple. I opened my eyes and regretted it, the harsh overhead lights stinging my retinas. I quickly snapped my eyelids shut and squeezed them, trying to even eliminate the orangy-pink glow through the skin.

"Tracy?" The deep familiar voice enveloped me with warmth.

I scrunched up my nose. My lips parted, but I realized immediately they were pruny and dry. I licked them but my tongue was like sandpaper.

"You need something to drink, sweetheart," the voice continued, and next thing I knew, there was a flexible plastic straw between my lips.

I took a tentative sip, then started gulping.

"Easy, we don't want you to choke," he said, pulling the straw back even as I leaned up to follow it.

A cool hand pressed my shoulder and pushed me back down–it was too small to be his hand. I knew his hands.

Nate.

I opened my eyes again, the light only slightly less offensive this time, and saw him sitting next to me, holding a plastic sipper with a straw poking out of the top.

The tubing coming out of my left arm pulled as I reached for the sipper. Or Nate. Or both.

What I wanted was in that direction, anyway.

Then I remembered the other hand. I turned my head and saw…

"Kinsley?" I mumbled. "What are you doing here? Come to think of it, where *is* 'here'? Weren't we on a plane to Ecuador?"

The two looked at each other.

"What?" I asked.

"Tracy," Nate said carefully, "do you remember getting kidnapped?"

"Kidnapped?" I frowned at him. "When did we get kidnapped?"

"On the plane." His voice was soft, coaxing memories out of me that he seemed to think I should have.

I looked at Kinsley. "Did Kinsley kidnap us?" I had to laugh. It was too ridiculous.

"No. She runs a special clinic for people who work outside the law," he replied.

"That's about as delicate as I've ever heard it put, Nate," she chuckled, bringing out the dimples the other girls at the finishing school had always teased her about.

I grinned at her familiar face. I mean, our teachers would have murdered her for her hair, make-up, piercings, tattoos, and the way she was dressed right now, but it suited her and I was glad she'd broken free of their chains. Probably years before me, as she was older. "Your dad finally let you go to med school?"

"Went without his permission. I sold my Aston Martin and used it to pay for my education. He was furious." Kinsley's smile was fond, until it fell. "It took him years to get back at me, but he did. He paid someone to file a malpractice suit against me. It wasn't my fault, but with my dad's lawyers, the patient won. But, I'm a skilled doctor and surgeon, and that doesn't go unnoticed. So, like Nate said, I care for people who work outside the law, now."

"Oh. Damn, your father is a real sonofabitch." She didn't deserve that kind of treatment.

"He was. He tried sniffing around my new place of employment when I didn't go running back home to be a good trophy wife. These aren't the kind of people or places a person should go sniffing around," she elaborated.

I swallowed. "Oh."

"It looked like a heart attack. We could still have an open casket and everything. Mother didn't know how it happened, but she was thrilled. I used my inheritance to set up this place. I think she's still in Barbados with a diving instructor." She shrugged. "That's what you get, I guess. No great loss. I felt a little bad about causing his death, but it passed when I remembered how he tried to ruin my life more than once."

"I-I see." I glanced at Nate. "So… if you're not holding us prisoner, who is?"

"Irena and Jacques. They were our flight attendant and pilot, respectively," he answered instead.

"They're in very high demand. Very professional. Phenomenal reputations," she said. "Very expensive. Someone must want you both very much."

With a heavy sigh, I dropped my spinning head into my hands. "It's becoming more of a novel than a list."

"You don't know who it is specifically?" she asked, blinking at us.

"No," we replied together.

"Damn. And I thought I was the prodigal daughter. What did you get yourself into?" Kinsley gaped.

Nate took my hand and squeezed it gently. "Are you up to telling Kinsley the story?"

"What about our captors?" I asked.

"They're in the sports bar."

He and I both stared at her. "They're where?"

"There's a kind of snack room with televisions in it that monitor the different patient rooms here—and the front and back entrances," she explained. "I'm sure they know you're awake, but I told them I'd come get them when you were able to be transported. Which won't be for at least twenty-four hours. I imagine they'll peek their heads in eventually, but for now they're letting me do my doctor thing."

I brushed my fingers over bandages on the side of my head, careful not to disturb anything. I didn't want the pain to worsen. The dull ache was bad enough. "What doctor things did you need to do to me?" I asked.

Kinsley waved a hand. "Not a whole lot. Your skull was fractured at your temple, which isn't great, but it was relatively easy to control the brain bleed. You've been resting nicely for three days."

"Three days?!" I gasped, sitting up again. The world spun and I groaned.

This time, Nate pushed me back against the pillows—something I might have enjoyed under different circumstances. "Please don't hurt yourself. I don't think I could go through that again."

I took a leaf from my Hatha yoga and began using breathing techniques to calm myself down. "I can't believe I was out for three days."

"You had a lot of healing to do," Kinsley said in her best bedside-manner tone.

My eyes narrowed. "It wasn't as easy as you're saying."

"Er..." Her cheeks heated up. "No."

"Did I almost die?" I asked both of them.

Kinsley bit her lip.

Nate sandwiched my hand between both of his. "It was more a question of brain damage, sweetheart."

Hatha yoga abruptly stopped working. "D-do I have brain damage?"

"No! No. You came through it all beautifully," she said.

"You did," he agreed.

"Then why am I missing time?" I demanded.

Kinsley sat down on the edge of the bed. "Brain injuries are sometimes like that. In fact, quite often. You hit your head when they were kidnapping you–before you even got off the plane. What is the last thing you remember?"

"I..." I thought back. It didn't take long. My last vivid memory was grinding in Nate's lap while his hands were on my breasts, both of us ignorant of anything happening on the plane. I wasn't even sure, at the time, if we'd taken off yet. I did know Nate tasted like dark chocolate and fine cigars and that if he didn't push up my skirt and open his pants soon, I was going to die. A primal need for him, even after a disappointing first time in his office. If it could have even been called that… "Um…"

"You are almost neon pink," she laughed. "Did you split your skirt getting on the plane or something and flash Nate?"

I'd have done that happily. "Not… um… exactly." I glanced at Nate.

He coughed, clearly understanding. "If *that's* your last memory, you didn't miss much. We were tranquilized. They got you after they got me, and Irena tells me you hit your head when you dropped."

"Irena… Jacques…" I vaguely remembered.

"Yes! Good, those are our kidnappers," he said encouragingly.

"I'm still curious about your last memory," Kinsley teased, giving my shoulder a gentle nudge. She leaned in by my ear. "Girl, I would let him screw my brains out, too. I mean, yum! Hello, daddy."

Certain I'd gone purple by now with embarrassment, I gave her a small, annoyed shove.

She laughed. "Okay, okay. But I really do want to hear the story."

"That's going to have to wait."

The three of us looked up and the woman I now recognized as Irena was standing in the doorway. She was holding a cell phone and looking annoyed. "The client has been informed about the damage to the package and has made arrangements. An equipped transport will be here shortly."

"I don't think it's a good idea to transport the patient at this time." Kinsley stood and inserted herself between Irena and the bed. "I told you I'd tell you when she was ready."

"The client has run out of patience. Get her prepped to go," Irena said.

"I must object—" Kinsley argued.

Irena slid a gun out of a leg holster and pointed it at Kinsley. "You're coming as well."

"What?!" Kinsley didn't even seem to see the weapon. She put her hands on her hips. "That's against code."

"Like how smuggling these two out later wouldn't have been against code? Admirable, but no. Besides, you will be compensated handsomely," Irena said. She pointed at me with her free hand. "Get her unhooked and ready to go, or I'll have Jacques do it."

Nate growled.

"Exactly. Doc, get a move on."

Kinsley looked insulted, but finally took her hands off her hips and got my I.V. taped up and the devices that were monitoring me unhooked.

When Jacques arrived moments later, Nate was already lifting me in his arms. The world spun despite his best efforts, and I thought I might throw up on him.

"Don't worry, sweetheart. I've got you," he murmured as he held me against his chest.

The feeling went away and I just laid my head on his shoulder.

"Same as before, try not to move her around too much," Kinsley said. "I'll keep an eye on her and check her when we get... wherever the fuck we're going." I could hear it in her voice that she was glaring at Irena.

Irena snorted.

Jacques ignored the whole thing. "The transport's here."

"Too bad. I'm going to miss the snacks," Irena replied.

I hid my face in Nate's shirt to block out the sight of things moving around me, feeling it was punishment enough.

He carried me straight for a while, then turned and we went out a door. I felt fresh air against my skin. I hazarded a glance and saw what looked like an unmarked ambulance.

"Set her here, sir," a man with a medical mask on said, pointing at the gurney outside of the open back doors of the ambulance.

Nate's arms tightened, but then relaxed as he reluctantly set me down.

The man and Kinsley then got me strapped in, Kinsley not looking

particularly happy about it, complete with a neck brace that immobi-
lized my head.

Then Kinsley and the man lifted the gurney and got me into the
back of the ambulance, collapsing its legs in the process.

"You're pretty good at this." The masked man nodded at Kinsley as
they got into the ambulance.

"It's an important skill to have," she replied, dusting off her hands.

Nate took a seat next to me, laying a hand on my arm. I was
grateful for it, and wished I could reciprocate.

Where did Irena and Jacques go? I wondered when the doors didn't
shut and the not-ambulance didn't move.

"It's a shame, really," the masked man sighed.

"What is?" she replied testily.

"Well—" I heard a strange rustling.

"No, don't!" Nate shouted.

Kinsley screamed.

There was a soft pop.

Something big and heavy fell on me.

And then Kinsley's lifeless eyes were staring into mine.

9

EVERYONE AROUND ME DIES

Nate

My heartbeat slowed as Kinsley's body fell. As Tracy was now conveniently covered by a human shield, I could react on instinct.

Before the masked man could turn his weapon on Tracy or me, I launched myself on him. He slammed into the wall of the ambulance with a loud 'oof.' I gripped his wrist and beat his hand against the wall until the gun clattered to the floor.

"You motherfucker," he hissed and tried to headbutt me, but I was ready for it and it didn't land.

Instead, I got him good in the stomach, and while he was doubled over in pain, trying to catch his breath, I grabbed his chin and the back of his head. *Just one hard jerk...*

A gun cocked. I turned my head to see Irena and Jacques outside, at the back of the ambulance.

"That's enough," Irena said sternly.

Jacques's gun was unwavering, perfectly aimed to put a hole in my head. With the cannon he was holding, he wouldn't even have to aim very well to blow my brains out.

I glanced at the gun on the floor of the ambulance.

"Don't do it," Irena warned me. "Don't be stupid. What's Tracy going to do if you're dead? You'll leave her all alone in this situation?"

A layer of enamel wore off my teeth as I ground them angrily. I gave a single, sharp shake of my head.

"I didn't think so. Now, let him go," she said.

Reluctantly, I released the masked man. He stumbled over to his gun and swept it up, pointing it at me, his eyes wild with fury.

"Dude, *we'll* kill you before we let you kill him. I'm sure our mutual employer will hunt you for the rest of your days if you do what you're thinking right now. Put on your professional panties and let's get the fuck out of here," Irena snapped.

The masked man's hand shook as he hesitated, but he finally lowered his weapon. "As soon as he's done with you, you're mine."

"Didn't know you were into S&M," I returned. "Not really my thing and, respectfully, I'm not into men. But, to each his own. I won't judge." Admittedly, not my most mature moment, but I'd had it up to my eyeballs with this whole affair.

He growled.

"Knock it off, both of you." Irena waved at the masked man. "Get in front with Jacques. You're too trigger happy to ride back here."

"But I'm a medical professional!" he protested.

"We'll pull over if there's a problem. Now go. I don't like hanging around chatting when there's a body stinking up the place. Getting a cop's attention is not on my list of things to do today," she said.

He stalked angrily to the back of the ambulance and jumped out, Jacques holding a gun on him the entire time.

Irena climbed in the back and closed the doors. "Sit."

I sat, letting the adrenaline work its way out of my body. Some of it, at least–it wasn't as though we were suddenly safe. Then, I noticed the whimpering Tracy was trying to suppress.

"Shit." I grasped Kinsley's lifeless body and moved it off Tracy.

Tracy was pale and covered in Kinsley's blood. If I hadn't known better, there was so much of it, I would have thought some of it was hers.

I touched her arm. "Sweetheart…" I wracked my brain for words of comfort.

"N-Nate," Tracy whispered, tears glistening in her eyes.

"Damn shame," Irena said, as Tracy's trembling lips fought to form words. "She was a great doctor."

I rounded on her. "Then why kill her?!"

"The client gave us evidence that she was making arrangements to get you out of the country. That's against the code," Irena explained. "You don't go against the code."

Tracy groaned as though in pain. "God, not again!"

"Sweetheart? Where does it hurt?" I asked, ignoring Irena for the moment.

"My heart," Tracy replied brokenly. She closed her eyes. "Oh God…" I touched her hair, careful to avoid any bandages.

"Is she having a heart attack?" Irena asked, leaning over.

"No, a flashback is more likely. Or just a bad memory," I said, as cool and calm as I would be in any boardroom. On the inside, however, my heart was breaking for Tracy. "Kinsley was a very good friend."

"So was Gwendolyn." Tracy's throat worked. She was holding back her emotions with all the strength she had. I gently massaged my fingers into her scalp.

"Tell me about Gwendolyn," I encouraged her as the ambulance's engine rumbled to life and we drove out of the alley.

"She was my friend," Tracy managed to choke out. "McKenzie and Will said… said they killed her by pouring acid down her throat. McKenzie heard it on the phone. She… we… we just wanted to help!"

"Oh, I know you did. I know. It just all spun out of control," I soothed. She needed to stay as calm as possible, and I was going to get her there.

Irena seemed to understand the mission and simply sat back on the bench on the other side of her, watching and listening. That part couldn't be helped.

"It did!" Tracy hiccuped. "It all spun out of control. All of it. And just when we thought we were safe, the Feds came for us because those *assholes* decided to take us down with them! And we didn't even do anything wrong!"

I stroked her cheek. "Go ahead and cry, sweetheart. You'll feel better."

The neck brace wriggled ever so slightly as she tried to shake her head.

"No, no, Tracy. You have to stay still." My touch became more firm.

"I won't cry. I won't give them the satisfaction," she said, her jaw set.

It wasn't as though I could fault her for the sentiment. I wouldn't have given them the satisfaction, either. However, it was the fastest way to get her calm. "Sweetheart," I whispered in her ear. "I need you to be ready for anything. Please cry for me. Let it out so you can be sharp when the time comes."

Her stubborn pout told me just how much she didn't want to. However, after a few minutes, she dissolved into soft sobs.

I kept stroking her—cheek, hair, arm. I murmured promises that I hoped to God I could deliver on.

"Stop here," Irena suddenly barked.

"You can't order me to stop crying," Tracy argued exactly what had been on the tip of my tongue.

"Not you. The ambulance," Irena sighed back as the ambulance came to a halt.

Jacques and the masked man jumped down and then the back doors opened. I frowned at the scene outside. It looked as though we were on the edge of a ravine in the middle of nowhere.

"Your client is picking us up here?" I asked.

"No, but we *are* making a drop off." Irena then grabbed the lifeless Kinsley and handed her off to the two men. "This is as good a place as any."

"What's happening?" Tracy asked.

So much for the calming down. I wasn't going to lie to her, though. "They're tossing Kinsley's body down a ravine," I said quietly.

"They're—no!" Tracy struggled in her restraints. "No, they can't!"

"Get her to sit still, Alton," Irena ordered. "I won't have her pulling her stitches on my watch."

"Maybe if you'd have waited until *after* you delivered us, this wouldn't have been a problem," I seethed. I turned to Tracy. "Sweetheart, it's okay. Someone will find her this way and she'll get a proper burial."

Jaques snorted. "Nah, the animals will get to her first."

"JACQUES!" Irena bellowed.

"Oh my God!" Tracy fought even harder against her restraints.

I decided (if the blessed time came) that Jacques was dying first, the sadistic bastard. "Tracy, sweetheart. Darling. Baby..." My endearments didn't work. She just kept getting more and more agitated.

Even the rocking of the ambulance getting back underway didn't quiet her. I began to fear she might really hurt herself, so I did the only other thing I could think of–I fused my lips to hers.

She bit me.

"Tracy!" I said, glad Jacques and the masked man had taken the body away and there was only Irena to witness my bleeding lip.

"What the fuck did you think you were doing?!" Tracy snapped while Irena covered her mouth. Her shoulders shook rather tellingly, however.

"I was trying to keep you from hurting yourself! What would Kinsley think, putting in all that effort to get you healthy again, only to have you mess up her work?" I asked.

The fight went out of her immediately as though I'd popped her balloon. "Oh."

"Yes. Oh." I sighed, wiped the blood off my lip, and gently kissed her forehead. "I'm sorry. I'm sorry about everything."

Tracy's eyes went suddenly vacant and I wondered for a terrible moment if she really had re-injured herself.

"Sweetheart?" I laid my hand against her cheek again. "Are you okay?"

"They're going to take you from me, too," she said, her voice hollow. "That's what they do. They kill everyone around you until there's nobody left." Her eyes welled up with tears. "I don't want to lose you, too."

"You won't." This fierce promise I would keep. I swore it in my soul. "I'll be there with you until the very end." I bumped my forehead to hers.

She swallowed. "What about your business?"

"Fuck my business," I replied without hesitation.

"What if they take your money?" she asked.

"Fuck that, too."

"What if you go to prison for helping me?"

"Then I go to prison."

Tracy closed her eyes. "They just want me. You should get yourself out, Nate."

"No."

She gave an exasperated huff. "You're so stubborn!"

"I'm told it's one of my best qualities," I smiled.

"In business, maybe, but this is your life!"

"Yes," I agreed. "This is my life, and my choice, and I choose to go through this with you."

Tracy looked lost. "Why?"

A loaded question, one I wasn't sure I knew the answer to at that time.

Luckily, the ambulance stopped and Irena stood. "I'm afraid that all's going to have to wait until later. We're here."

The back doors swung open and six new men, in suits with ear pieces, flanked each side. With them were two additional men in white coats who I could only assume were doctors.

"The boss will see you now," the closest security guard on the right said in a gravelly voice.

"Great. I'd love to see the boss," I replied. But I didn't move–not without Tracy.

Both doctors moved forward. "Please step out of the ambulance. We need room to move her."

I eyed all of them, then reluctantly stepped down, as did Irena. The doctors then bustled the gurney out of the ambulance.

While they began checking Tracy over, I took in our new surroundings. We were near the end of a long drive leading to a stately, white mansion I didn't recognize, complete with Grecian columns at the entrance. Wide, lush green lawns and gardens, perfectly manicured, spread out around it. A large fountain occupied the center of the circular drive in front of the mansion. And, aside from the security surrounding us, I could see several more stationed around the grounds. I'd assumed so before, but now it was confirmed: the client who had bought us had a good deal of money.

When I looked back, Tracy was off the gurney and seated in a wheelchair. "You okay, sweetheart?"

"Yes. I got a little dizzy getting down, but I'm okay now," she responded. She reached for my hand.

I took it without hesitation. "Remember, I'm going to make it okay." She nodded, though whether or not she believed that was possible at this point, I wasn't sure.

What I was sure of was that this was going to come down to money–everything always did–and I had a lot of it.

"Now, Nate. Why are you lying to the poor girl?" a new, familiar voice asked.

I whirled around, then stared openmouthed at my ex-business partner–who'd embezzled from me, and was supposed to be dead.

"Fuck me–Owen?" I gaped.

10

THE JADE'S TRICK

Tracy

This is not a good person. I could tell by the tension in Nate's jaw and the hard squeeze of his hand. *This is not a good person!*

Owen, blond with an athletic build and a smile that could charm the pants off Joan of Arc, opened his arms. "It's been ages, Nate. Why don't we bring it in, as the kids say."

Nate did not so much as move a toe in his direction.

Dropping his arms, Owen still didn't lose his smile. "Ouch. Is that any way to treat your partner?"

"Ex." Nate's voice dripped venom.

"Semantics." Owen looked down at our joined hands. "Ah. I see. Does Lillian know you're sleeping with her daughter? Tsk, tsk, what a cliche. And you who always said cradle robbing was beneath you."

Nate didn't lower himself to answer him. I was rather proud of that and threaded my fingers through his in solidarity.

"I did hear she finally left you. I seem to remember trying to warn you about Lillian. But banging her behind your back was awfully satisfying, too. I had her on your wedding night, did you know that? That was…" He blew a chef's kiss.

Shit. I looked up at Nate. It was something I had no trouble believing of my mother, but it was something he never deserved. He was a good man. "It's okay," I said softly, rubbing my thumb over his palm as his whole body vibrated with tension. "She's not worth it—and neither is he."

Nate stayed tense for another few moments, then relaxed and gave my hand a squeeze.

Owen's lips thinned, clearly disappointed he hadn't gotten a rise out of him. Then a twinkle of mischief returned to his eyes and my stomach dropped. Something very bad was about to come out of his mouth, I just knew it. "Is that pussy as good as mommy's? Should I find out?"

The first question would have been enough. The second was complete overkill. Nate let go of my hand. I grabbed for his wrist, but touched nothing but air. He was just too fast!

That was Owen's mistake as well. He hadn't understood just how fast Nate could be—much faster than his security guards.

Nate gripped Owen by the throat and slammed him to the ground. "You don't touch her," he snarled. "You don't *ever* touch her!"

Owen gurgled helplessly, clawing Nate's arm and wrist, until security pulled Nate off of him seconds later. Owen coughed while four security guards held Nate down on the ground.

"Damn. You were never that feral over Lillian," Owen croaked. He accepted a hand up from another member of his security team and went to loom over Nate. "Never knew you had that in you. I guess it's true that being with a younger woman makes you feel young."

I was uneasy, watching Nate on the ground. He didn't answer Owen this time and looked only at me. I didn't want to be a weak point for Owen to use, however. I straightened up in my wheelchair. "It's not like that. He's helping me. He felt sorry for me, that's all. He just thinks of me as a lost kid."

My lie completely unraveled in one snort from Irena, who I'd forgotten was still there—probably waiting for her payment. "From what I saw on the plane, sir, he doesn't think of her as anybody's kid."

Owen snickered. "Nice try."

I tried changing tactics. "He doesn't know anything. If you guys were friends, you can just let him go and do whatever you want with me."

"Fuck that," Nate growled. "I know every goddamn thing."

"I very much doubt that. Tracy isn't even the biggest fish in her little group. *That* one got away from us," Owen sighed. "*She* hardly knows anything of importance, but it's always that little bit that can bite you right in the ass."

"Please. The FBI is in your back pocket. You might as well have Will," I scoffed.

Owen smiled. "Yes. But not Caleb."

"For the—what more do you intend to do to that poor man?!" I shook my head and instantly regretted it. I pressed forward anyway. "He's practically a grandpa! You've been after him for, like, two-thirds of his life!"

"He's a slippery little bastard, I'll give him that," Owen said.

"He's been permanently disfigured and lost someone he considers his son! *Twice!* And that's just the top of the list! You heartless, soulless, fucking asshole!" Now I was the one trembling with anger.

Owen rubbed two fingers together. "Here's the world's smallest violin playing just for Caleb–and the rest of you. I am a heartless, soulless, fucking asshole. You'll do well to remember that." He turned back to Nate. "What to do with you..."

"I'll give you whatever you want if you let her go to my house in Ecuador. She'll be outside the law then, and practically removed from civilization altogether. She can't hurt you there," Nate said. "You can do whatever you want with me..."

The hell with that! "I'll give you whatever you want," I jumped in quickly. "Just name it."

Owen's speculative eyes raked over me, ignoring Nate for now. "You don't have a lot to give, I'm afraid. I've been in better bodies than yours. Granted, not many, but a few. I don't have to bargain with them. Technically, I wouldn't have to bargain with you, either. I think you are both mistaken in thinking you have some sort of power here." His smile sent chills down my spine as he walked over and gripped my chin. "I can take whatever I want."

I braced myself, expecting him to kiss me. Instead, he turned my head and licked my cheek all the way up to my hairline on my good side. My stomach turned in revulsion.

"Leave her the fuck alone, Owen!" Nate yelled.

He smiled, and I could see I'd played right into his hands. He didn't want to toy with me at all. He wanted to toy with Nate. He was going to dangle me over Nate's head to do it. "Aww, Nate, you never let me have any fun. No wonder I had to take all your money and leave."

"Owen, I swear to God—"

"No," Owen interrupted him. "You don't swear to God. You don't swear to Peter or Paul or even Satan. It's not going to help you." He grinned at me. "I think I'll bang her right in front of you."

"No!" Nate bellowed.

Owen nodded to the security guards, who dragged Nate up into a kneeling position. The asshole leaned down by Nate's ear, but still spoke loud enough for his audience to hear. "What *would* you do to keep her safe? Hm? Mr. Holier-Than-Thou? Mr. Boyscout? What terrible, horrible atrocities would you be willing to commit?"

Nate remained silent.

"I think I'd like to find out." Owen held out a hand to one of the security guards. The guard handed over his sidearm without a moment's hesitation. I held my breath as Owen then turned the gun on Nate.

"Please, don't!" I begged.

Owen grinned at me. "Tracy, don't worry. I'm going to do something so much worse." *Worse?!* I stared at him, then gasped when he turned the gun and pressed the butt of it into Nate's hand.

"Don't get excited. These men here have orders to riddle both of you with bullets if you so much as point that gun at me," Owen said to Nate. He nodded to the guards, who pulled Nate to his feet.

Nate kept the gun pointed at the ground, his eyes wary.

Owen withdrew a gun from his jacket and pressed the barrel to Nate's temple. "Shoot the mercenaries."

"Wait, what?" Jacques said while Irena turned to run.

It was over before I could blink. With two loud bangs, both Jacques and Irena were gone.

"Nice aim, Wild Bill. I didn't want to pay them anyway. And who knew what they knew?" Owen nodded again and the man in the mask was hauled out from behind a tree several yards down the lawn. "Can you hit him at that distance?"

Nate raised the gun and fired, and the masked man went down.

"That's great! Let's try someone a little more challenging, shall we?" Owen looked at one of the men guarding me.

I knew Nate would die before shooting me, just as I would die before shooting him. I didn't know much more about our relationship, but mutual respect and not shooting each other were at least pillars of it. There was a big vat of lust under those pillars, but I didn't question them for a minute.

The guard touched his ear. "Bring out the kid."

Kid? Oh no. No-no-no-no-no-no. I glanced around, wondering where this kid was going to pop out from.

They marched him around the side of the house—sweaty, panicking, and crying. He wasn't a 'kid' exactly. He was maybe four years my junior, but at least twenty for sure. "I'm sorry, Mr. Jorgensen! It won't happen again!"

"Of course it won't, Trevor. Do you think I'd let you make that same mistake again?" Owen snorted. "I told you when you started working for me that if you ever crossed me, this is what would happen."

"I was going to pay you back. I promise! I still will!" Trevor insisted, shaking from head to toe as the guard brought him up to stand between Nate and me.

"Yes, I know. And this is how you're going to do it." Owen turned to Nate. "Kill him."

Trevor looked at Nate and must have seen a killer there because his knees gave. He knelt on the ground in front of Owen, who still had a gun to Nate's head, and Nate, who hadn't lifted his an inch. "Sir, I'm sorry. I'm sorry," he blubbered. "I did wrong, I know that. Please don't kill me. Please."

"Nate…" Owen had a warning tone. "I told you to kill him."

"No," Nate replied. "I won't."

"Then I'm going to shoot you, Nate," Owen said, pressing the gun harder into Nate's temple.

"No…" I begged. I actually begged the asshole. "Please, I'll do anything—"

"We already had this conversation. You're going to do 'anything' anyway." Owen gave me a disconcerting smile. "But I do know how to up the ante. Sanders?"

The man who'd called for Trevor unbuckled his gun and put it to my good temple.

Nate's eyes went wide. He looked at Trevor.

"Don't do it," I said quickly. "Don't. Don't do it, Nate. It's okay. It's okay if I don't make it, but you can't do this."

"Oh, I think he can," Owen smirked. "Care to make a wager?"

"I'm not betting on a man's life!" I snapped.

Trevor crawled across the grass and grabbed Nate's pants with both fists. "Please don't shoot me. Please. I'm not the greatest guy, but I don't deserve to die. I promise. I'll be better. I'll go join the priesthood! Whatever you want."

Nate didn't move. He just looked at me.

Owen sighed. "I suppose I'll just have to kill her then." He signaled to the guard beside me.

I closed my eyes.

"Stop," Nate barked.

I opened my eyes. "Nate?"

Owen held up a hand. "Yes, Mr. Boyscout?"

Nate looked steadily at me. Then, I saw it in his eyes.

"No, Nate—!" I screamed.

Nate put the gun to the top of Trevor's head and fired.

11

BLOOD ON MY HANDS

Nate

I couldn't look at her. I lowered the gun to my side and lowered my eyes to the grass that was already splattered with Trevor's blood, bone, and brain matter. I couldn't look at her.

"Well, that was exciting!" Owen said pleasantly.

Fuck, I wanted to shoot him more than I'd ever wanted to shoot anyone in my entire life. But I knew there were still guns on us, most notably the one pointed right at Tracy's head.

Owen took the gun from me and handed it back to its owner. "I didn't think you had it in you, Nate. Good job!" He clapped me on the back. "All right, folks. Show's over. Let's get these lovebirds to their nest, shall we?" He stepped over Trevor's corpse as though it were merely a large pile of dog shit and started toward Tracy.

I grabbed his arm. Hard. "Don't."

He rolled his eyes at me. "Jesus, Nate. I was just going to hand her my handkerchief. You made her cry."

I made her cry. I felt sick. Well, sick-er. Pulling the trigger and killing Trevor had already made me want to throw up. I was going to hate myself for a long time for that. Maybe forever.

"Nate, let go," Owen said, sounding less pleasant. "I will make sure all sorts of bad things happen to her if you don't."

Reluctantly, I released him. He strode confidently over to Tracy and pulled a handkerchief out of the jacket of his sport coat. I couldn't see her face, but I did see her arm as she tossed the handkerchief on the ground beside her wheelchair, without using it. A flicker of pride almost pushed away my guilt…almost.

"You are both impossible," Owen sighed. He reached out.

I couldn't see exactly what he was doing, but she slapped his hand away. I took a step forward, sure he'd touched her, but I was stopped immediately by security.

Owen laughed. "Come now, Tracy. Don't you want to be my good girl?"

"Not even if hell froze over!" she spat.

He moved aside and her eyes sought mine, but I lowered my gaze. I didn't want to see what was inside them.

"You two are going to be fun," he grinned.

"Go to hell," she replied tightly.

Owen chuckled. "Let's go." He turned and headed for the mansion.

One of the guards wheeled Tracy after him while one walked on either side of her chair, treating her as though my injured girl might jump up and show off some ninja moves at any moment. The thought would have made me smile twenty minutes ago. Just twenty minutes ago, when I was someone else–someone I recognized.

I had four guards in a diamond formation around me, rightfully cautious of me. When we got to the five steps it would take to reach the front door, I frowned and looked at her guards. They'd stopped the wheelchair at the bottom of the steps and one guard was crouching to lift her out of the chair.

Tracy kicked him in the balls.

"Fuck!" the guard grunted, stepping back. "Jesus, woman, I'm just trying to get you in the goddamn house!"

"Don't you fucking touch me!" she snapped.

Owen paused at the door and turned around. "Miss Franz. I think you want to be a bit more cooperative. And polite… There will be consequences for your actions, and I don't think you'll like them very much."

She scowled at him. "You can take your consequences and—"

"I'll carry her," I said quickly.

He turned to me, a slow, diabolical smile spreading across his face. "What an excellent suggestion. Yes, I think that will solve all our problems."

I didn't wait for any more commentary from him. I pushed one of my guards aside and walked over to her.

Tracy lifted her arms without me having to ask, and I scooped her up and held her against me while she wound her arms around my neck. Fuck me, but she was balm for my ragged soul, even just like this. I closed my eyes and breathed.

A guard laid a heavy hand on my shoulder, a warning and also to remind me we weren't alone.

"See? No fuss, no muss." Owen led the way into the house.

One guard carried the wheelchair up the steps while I carried Tracy. When we got inside, he gestured for me to put her back down.

Her arms tightened around my neck. "No," she said.

The guard frowned. "Sir?"

Owen grinned, looking very entertained. "Just let it be for now."

I noticed he was standing under a large chandelier in the foyer and had a deep desire to go Phantom of the Opera on his ass, but I also wasn't some stupid kid anymore. The main objective was to keep Tracy safe. So, for now, I was going to go along and get along.

"Do you want the tour?" Owen smirked.

"You're not going to give me the tour. You don't want me to know where the exits are," I replied.

He laughed. "You always were sharp, Nate. All right. This way."

I still got to see a good deal of the main floor as he led us, still surrounded by guards, through the mansion and out a side door. There I saw a large pool with a pool house to one side.

"Tada!" he said, gesturing to the pool house. "Welcome to your cage."

Tracy's head came up and she studied the 'cage' with me. I didn't think it would be too difficult to escape. I forced myself not to smile.

Owen, apparently psychic, grinned. "I'd love to see you get out of this one. Allow me to give you the tour."

"Fine," I said, sounding nonchalant.

He was almost giddy as we walked inside, which gave me a bad feeling. As soon as the last guard crossed the threshold, the front door slammed shut with an ominous low beep and steel rods slid across the frame, effectively locking us inside.

Frustration bubbled inside me. "Nice touch."

"Both doors and all the windows are also rigged with alarms. If you did manage to get one open—which is a very unlikely scenario— you wouldn't get far, because half the guards on my property would be on you in seconds. Plus I have guards patrolling this area at all times. You will, of course, be fed, but if you could refrain from killing my housekeeper when she comes to bring you dinner, that would be appreciated." He winked.

I thought of Trevor and felt sick with self-loathing. "I have no intention of killing anyone else."

"We'll see." He continued the tour. "Bathroom. Living area. Kitchen. And, most important for you two, the bedroom."

"Just one?" I asked, glancing around.

"Why would you need more than one? The bed's big enough, and you're going to be screwing her brains out anyway. I'm jealous. Maybe I'll decide to have a taste." He licked his lips lewdly.

Tracy's nails dug into the back of my neck.

Mentally, I took back what I said. I was going to kill someone else. I was going to kill him.

Owen burst out laughing. "The look on your faces!"

"Ha-ha," I growled.

She glared at him. "The day you touch me is the day you lose your balls, asshole."

"I'm sure you'd like to think so." He snickered and led us into the bedroom. "I figured you might want to put her down."

The bed was, indeed, spacious. But I was reluctant to let go of her.

"Aw, that's so sweet. Look at Nate, all protective," he cooed. "You weren't ever this gaga over Lillian. But then, I suppose you were never in a situation like this with her mother."

"Are we done with the tour?" I asked tightly.

"Almost." He turned to the closet and slid the door open. "Fresh clothes and towels. Margarite has you well-stocked. I did, however, fail to see just how boobalicious our Tracy here is, so the shirts might be a little tight."

My jaw tensed. "You can keep your eyes off her anatomy."

"Exactly!" she agreed. Her arms were still wrapped tightly around me. She didn't want to get down, either.

"But it's such lovely anatomy," he teased.

He wanted a rise out of me—out of *us*. I wasn't going to give it to him. I gave her a warning squeeze as well. Her nails dug into my neck again, but she didn't say a word.

"You two are no fun." He waved a hand at the guards. "All right, men. Let's leave these two alone."

"I'm assuming you're with them," I said, making him pause.

"Of course I am. I thought that much was obvious." He rolled his eyes.

"So, you took my money and used it for human trafficking, drugs, illegal weapons sales, and God knows what else?" I asked.

Owen grinned. "I like to think of it as 'our' money—but yes, I did exactly that. How does it feel to know money you made was used for such things?"

It made my blood boil. "I'm sure I don't have to tell you."

He laughed.

"You could have just taken your half," I said.

"That wouldn't have been enough to seal the partnership with Masterson," he responded. "Sorry, not sorry."

"Masterson?" Tracy sounded sick. "Partner?"

"Silent partner," he confirmed. "You and your friends have made my life quite difficult. Luckily, I can rebuild. Of course, it would be nice if Will contributed some capital…"

She snorted. "My brother will never do that."

Owen raised an eyebrow. "Brother, hm? I suppose Lillian was tramping around with Will Sr.?"

"Masterson was a monster. Will's father didn't 'tramp around.' He was a hero," she said vehemently.

"Ah. So Masterson made himself a proper heir the new-fashioned way." He nodded to himself. "Too bad Will didn't match his expectations. In fact, he's a real pain in the ass."

"Good," she shot back.

He chuckled. "All right, well, I'll leave you two to get settled. We'll talk more later. Oh, and don't get too frisky, Nate. She's still got a head injury, after all."

I wasn't at all worried about that. Tracy wasn't ever going to see me that way again. "I will pay you whatever you want to let her go."

"And I don't want or need your money. I want you both silenced," he replied.

Tracy stiffened in my arms. "Are you going to kill us?"

"Of course," he laughed. "Of course I am. But I want to have a little fun first."

"Owen..." I began. "You can't..."

"I assure you, I can. And by the time I'm finished with your high and mighty ass, you'll be a broken shell of a man who would lick my shoes if it meant she took one more breath. You're nine-tenths of the way there already," he said flatly.

I frowned. "I don't know what I did to make you hate me this much, but I can tell you do. If this is about you and me..."

"It's about all you lousy do-gooders and your holier-than-thou attitudes. When it comes down to it, you'll all lower yourselves into the mud with the rest of us," he responded, his eyes gleaming with fury.

He was insane. Owen was absolutely, one hundred percent insane! "That doesn't make sense—"

"Don't worry. It will later." He smiled at us and I couldn't help but think it was a little crazed. "I'll be off now. The black market waits for no man."

Then, he left whistling as though he'd just finished paying a welcome visit.

The guards left with him, leaving just Tracy and me.

Alone.

12

LOOK AT ME

Tracy

As far as I could tell, Nate had completely forgotten he was holding me, there in the middle of the bedroom. He'd just completely… frozen.

I waited in the silence that Owen's absence had left for what must have been nearly ten minutes, then awkwardly reached up and touched Nate's cheek. "Nate? Are you okay?" Alright, it was a stupid question. How were either of us okay in this situation?

He snapped out of it. "Right. Yes. I need to take stock of our supplies and check out the situation with the locks. I don't think there will be an easy way out, but you never know." He carefully deposited me on the bed and tucked a pillow under my head. "You just stay here. I'll be right back."

Nate still didn't look at me. I'd noticed him avoiding my eyes ever since he shot Trevor. "Nate?"

"It's going to be okay. I'm going to fix this." He patted my hand and all but ran from the room.

"Nate!" I protested, but he didn't come back. I could see him occasionally through the door as he moved through the pool house like a whirlwind, checking cupboards in the kitchen, passing through the living room and examining the furniture in there. Back and forth. I figured he was also checking the doors and windows.

He paused at the bedroom door, then gave a soft knock. "I'm going to check in here, too."

Still no eye contact. "Okay…"

Nate stepped into the room and began examining every piece of decor, from picture frames to fake shells. He systematically went through the contents of the closet—his and mine—and separated them into piles, feeling along the seams of sleeves and even the thongs of my underwear. *Thong underwear*, I grimaced. *Great.*

The back of his neck flushed while he was doing it. "Tracking devices," he explained as though apologizing.

"Found any yet?" I asked.

"Yes."

"Really? Where?"

He just held up my underwear and one of his shirts.

"*Seriously?!* Isn't that kind of overkill? I mean, he has us trapped here like hamsters," I huffed.

"There's a device sewn into every piece of clothing so far," he said. "And yes, it is overkill, in my opinion. I've seen the locks."

"No easy escape, then," I sighed.

"No." He carefully folded our clothes and put them back in the closet. He sat back on his heels and dropped his head into his hands. "Shit."

I leaned up on my elbows. "Hey. I know people who've gotten out of worse situations than this. Don't lose hope, all right?"

Nate looked up, then quickly looked away. "Of course not. There's always hope."

I rolled on one side and reached out a hand. "Nate?"

His lips pressed together as he looked at my hand. "That's not a good idea, Tracy."

"Why?" I didn't stop reaching for him.

"Because I'm not a good person." He turned away.

I dropped my hand. "Why do you think that?"

"Tracy, I just killed three people. Did you not see that?" he said bitterly.

"Yes." In fact, I remembered quite vividly, but that didn't stop me from reaching for him again. "Come here."

He shook his head. "No."

My eyes stung and I panicked, suddenly feeling shut out and alone, my only ally turning his back on me. "Please?" My voice cracked.

Nate turned back. He hesitated, then came over to me, eyes downcast. He took my hand. "It's okay, Tracy. I'm still here. And I will be until we find a way out."

"And after?" I asked. I clung to his hand, hating myself a bit for it, but also desperate enough not to let go.

"After? I get you to Ecuador and then go deal with the authorities back in Minnesota," he said.

"Oh," I responded. "Okay."

He rubbed his thumb along the back of my hand. "I need to clear your name, Tracy—and your friends'. That was always the plan, remember?"

I looked up at him, but he still wouldn't meet my eyes. "Nate, I need you to look at me."

"I'm afraid I can't do that, Tracy," he grunted.

I swallowed, my heart squeezing in my chest. "Please?" Something in my breaking voice must have convinced him because his chocolate brown eyes finally flicked to mine. I tugged his arm to bring him down to my level so he was kneeling on the floor, not breaking eye contact for a second. "You are not a bad man," I said fiercely.

Nate winced. "Tracy, you saw..."

"I saw a good man in a bad situation," I interrupted him. "That's all."

He stared at me and searched my eyes. I hoped he would see the truth there. "You're serious."

"Of course I am!" I took his hand in both of mine and held it to my chest. "None of that was your fault. It's Owen's fault. He might as well have been holding the gun himself."

"But…" He tried looking away again, but I grabbed his chin. The pain in his eyes broke my heart. "Weren't you afraid of me? Aren't you now?"

"I was…" I wasn't going to lie to him. "I was scared at the time, but I wasn't after."

"Why not after?"

I rubbed my cheek against his hand. "Because it's *you*. How could I ever be afraid of you?" Nate's eyes did their melty chocolate thing and I knew what he wanted even if he wasn't going to ask.

"Yes," I said softly. His lips parted and I remembered them on my breasts. I let go of his hand so I could pull up my shirt.

"Fuck," he breathed, staring at my chest.

"I hope so," I replied.

He squeezed his eyes shut. "Sweetheart, you don't know what you're asking for."

"I do," I said. "I'm asking for you."

That broke his resolve. "We… we have to be careful. Your concussion."

"You will be," I assured him.

"Fuck." He stood, then leaned over me and helped me get my shirt the rest of the way off. Then he unsnapped my bra and drew it down my arms. His hand was warm and rough as he palmed one of my breasts. "Jesus, you're so perfect, sweetheart." I shivered as he rubbed a calloused thumb over my nipple. "So sensitive, too." He licked his lips and I knew what he wanted to do—instead, his hand traveled down my body. He tickled my stomach and I giggled. He smiled, then his hand traveled lower, over my skirt, and down my thigh. Then, without warning, he pushed his hand up under my skirt and flicked the flimsy strip of underwear between my legs aside. Before I knew it, his fingers were inside me.

"Nate!" I cried, my hips bucking off the mattress.

"Shh, easy. Let me take care of you." He got on the bed with me and held me down with one big hand low on my stomach. I whimpered, his fingers causing a confusing number of sensations; I didn't know if I was sore or if I felt good. He lowered his head and sucked my nipple into his mouth, swirling his tongue around it in a completely indecent way.

My body decided I felt good–really good. So good, in fact, that I had my first male-induced orgasm–the pleasure making me cry out as my inner muscles clamped around his fingers.

"Good girl," he murmured. "Now, just let me do all the work. I've got you." He took off every stitch of clothing I had left, leaving me naked on the bed. Then he started taking off his own.

I'd seen him naked before, but hadn't really appreciated the view. This time, I took in every inch of his muscular body. He clearly took good care of himself. My mouth actually watered.

His hands stopped at the waistband of his silk boxers, which were tented by his hard dick. "Don't be scared," he said. "I'm going to be very gentle."

"Why would I be scared?" I responded. "I've seen it before."

"Yes, but I also hurt you with my cock before, so I don't want you to worry about that again," he explained.

"But, I mean, it's still going to hurt a little bit, right?" I asked.

Nate gave a sad half-smile. "It might, but not as bad as before. I'm going to do everything in my power to make this good for you."

"Then that's fine. You're not going to traumatize me if you take off your boxers," I grinned.

"Tease," he chuckled.

"I'm only a tease if I don't deliver. You're a tease," I laughed. "Now, drop 'em."

He winked at me and hooked his fingers in the waistband of his boxers. "You asked for it."

"Absolutely," I agreed.

Nate shoved his boxers to the floor then kicked them aside. His cock bobbed big and proud, waving happily at me.

I did have an oh-my-God-am-I-really-letting-him-put-that-monster-inside-me-again moment.

"You should see the look on your face." He sat down on the edge of the bed. "Still game? We can do other things if you're not."

"Preeetty sure that's not going to fit in my mouth any better than it will other places," I said with a swallow. "But… yes. I'm still game. You said you'd be gentle and I want to be with you so there has to be a first time."

"I like that you agree we're going to have sex on several occasions," he replied. "But technically, this is our second time."

"Not to me."

He drew a shuddering breath. "Oh sweetheart. You do this old man's heart good."

I snorted. "Old man my ass."

"I am old enough to be your father," he reminded me.

"So? What, you want me to call you 'daddy' while you screw my brains out?" I teased.

Nate's eyes darkened and a white bead of precum appeared at the tip of his cock and trickled down the side. I reached out and ran a finger down its path, curious about the feel of him. Then, as he was still trembling from my touch, I popped my finger in my mouth. "Not too bad."

"Fuck me," he groaned. Suddenly, he was on the floor again, kneeling next to the bed.

"Okay, strange development, what are you—*eek!*" He grabbed my legs and pulled me to the edge of the bed, my legs dangling over the side. I gasped when he spread my knees. "Y-you're not seriously—"

"Oh, I am seriously. I like your taste-testing idea." He licked his lips. "I'll bet you taste like candy."

"Candy?" I panted as he spread me open with his thumbs.

"Hard candy. The kind you have to really suck on to get the sweetness," he rumbled. It was a promise that made me start to pant. Then his tongue was inside me and I cried out in surprise.

He slung my legs over his shoulders, settling in for a leisurely session of eating me out. At first it felt weird, but then, so had his fingers. Then, as with his fingers, things started to feel really… really good.

While I made sounds I didn't recognize, he reached up and pinched my nipple and sucked roughly on my clit. I came hard against his mouth, my fingers tangling in his hair. My scream of pleasure echoed around us. "*Daddy!*"

Nate groaned as he licked me clean. "Yes, sweetheart," he said in a guttural tone once he'd finished. "I'm your daddy now."

"Yes," I moaned, my whole body satiated and hungry at the same time. "God, yes, daddy, whatever you want."

"I want you." He got me back on the bed, then prowled up between my legs. He lined himself up at my entrance, dripping with the same need I felt. He took one of my hands and twined his fingers with mine. "Are you ready, sweetheart?"

I nodded. "If you don't fuck me now, I might die."

He chuckled. "Well, we can't have that, can we? What a waste that would be." Then he pushed his hips forward and the head of him eased inside me. I gasped and dug my nails into his shoulder. My other hand squeezed his.

"It's okay, sweetheart. Daddy's got you." He kept slowly inching his way into me.

Just when I thought that dick of his was never going to end, he was in all the way. He stroked my cheek. "I'm in. I'm going to start soon, but I wanted to make sure that you're okay."

"I'm okay, daddy," I whispered after taking stock. "I'm full, but it's okay."

I felt him shiver when I called him 'daddy.' "It's going to be more than okay in a minute," he promised. He gave me the softest of kisses. "Wrap your legs around my waist." I did as he asked, kissing him as I crossed my ankles behind his back. Then he did the most incredible thing: He started to move.

"Mm," I said, biting my lip against more of the crazy sounds I'd been making before.

Nate wasn't having any of that. He popped my lip back out from between my teeth with some gentle pressure from his thumb. "I want to hear you moan," he murmured hotly.

"Okay, daddy." God, I was going to be embarrassed later, but when he used that tone, I'd have happily done anything he wanted.

"That's right. I'm your daddy." He thrust a little harder and faster. I moaned for him; my arm wrapped around his neck, my other hand still gripping his. It felt... sore–that was there, but he also did things with his dick that sent sparks through my entire body.

He was being careful, I could tell. Distantly, I wondered what kind of frenzied coupling we'd have been having if I didn't have a concussion. Probably on every piece of furniture in the pool house. I shivered at the thought.

"Daddy's close, sweetheart," he said, his voice strained. "Just... give me... a second..." Nate detangled his hand from mine and I made a sound of protest. "Shh," he whispered, kissing me. "Just a second."

He reached between our coupling bodies and rubbed my clit while he pumped in and out of me.

I swore I saw fireworks. I yowled—actually yowled—and came around his cock, my inner muscles just as eager to fist around his dick as they were his fingers. It felt fucking fantastic!

"That's right, sweetheart. Milk daddy." He groaned and I felt his hot cum pulse into me.

13

—————

HARD CANDY

Nate

"D-daddy," Tracy said, teeth chattering as her body slowly calmed down.

I rolled to the side and wrapped her in my arms, still inside her. Still hard. Damn it. "Did I make you feel good?" I asked to distract myself, kissing her hair.

She swatted my shoulder. "You know you did. Are you going to act all proud now?"

I laughed and kissed her stubborn nose. "I am a bit proud, actually."

"You came, right?" she asked, her cheeks flushing. I kissed those, too. "I mean, like, inside I felt—"

"I came," I assured her. "You made me feel good, too."

"But you're still hard," she managed, her blush deepening.

"I am." I slid a hand between us and fondled her breast. Damn, she had the most perfect breasts.

Tracy trembled and I felt the little flutter of her muscles around my cock. "Nate..."

"Will you let me go again? I can't make any promises because you make me feel like a teenage boy, but it might go down the next time I come." I nuzzled her ear.

She answered by locking her legs around my waist and kissing my shoulder. "Okay, daddy."

I groaned and grabbed her ass as I rolled her onto her back, fighting to push deeper inside her. "Sweetheart, if you keep calling me that, I'm going to lose my fucking mind!"

Her tits rubbed against my chest as she wrapped her arms around my neck. There wasn't a breath of space between our bodies. I liked it.

"You say that like it's a bad thing, daddy," she replied innocently.

My dick got painfully hard, buried deep in the warm wetness of her body.

Tracy blinked at me. "Did you just get bigger?"

"Yes. Ah, fuck." I rocked my hips, trying to find some relief with a little friction. I could tell from the way she nearly went cross-eyed that she liked the gentle rocking, too. "Fuck, I have to remember you still have that concussion…" Reluctantly, I began to pull out. "I can take care of this in the bathroom. I'll just—"

She dug her nails into my back. "Please fuck me, daddy," she begged. Whatever resolve I'd managed to muster disappeared in a blink. I shoved my cock back into her ready hole. We both moaned.

"Sweetheart, you're going to be so sore later," I murmured, palming her breast and rubbing my thumb back and forth over her nipple. This did not stop me from thrusting into her body over and over again. At this point, no amount of guilt would stop me from having her.

Soft lips brushed my neck as she panted against my skin. "It's okay, daddy."

"I might not be able to stop at just one more time," I warned her– or, rather, informed her. There was no going back now.

"I know, daddy." She touched my cheek. I looked into those ocean blue eyes filled with desire and something else, and felt as though I could climb mountains. I kissed her hungrily, all the while thrusting desperately into her body as though coming inside her could absolve me of my sins.

"It's okay, daddy. I've got you," she said as though reading my mind. That nearly sent me right over the edge. I squeezed her breast, then worked my hand down between our bodies to toy with her clit. She gasped. "I'm close, sweetheart," I breathed in her ear. "Let's get you there, too."

"I'm—" She cried out and clamped down on my cock. Her perfectly manicured nails cut into my back and the tiny sharp pain had me coming hard.

"That's my good girl," I groaned as her muscles milked my dick. I came for a long time, finding absolution between her legs.

Tracy's breaths came in short little bursts, and I could tell she was tired, but she held me just the same while I kept releasing inside her. She played with the hair at the nape of my neck and it sent a calming sensation all the way down my spine.

Finally, I finished. This time, I carefully pulled out and rolled onto my back. My cock had gone down for the most part, though the bastard was just hard enough to remind me he'd be happy to go again. I ignored him and gathered her to me, pillowing her head on my shoulder as I wrapped her in my arms.

With natural ease, she draped her arm over my abdomen and snuggled against me. Her leg came to rest between mine. "Daddy?" she asked.

My dick perked up immediately. I swallowed. "Yes, sweetheart?"

She ran her finger down my cock, from tip to base. "You still look like you need me."

I caught her wrist, trying hard to calm myself down. "You're concussed; you've given me more than I could possibly have dared to ask for. I can handle this."

"But—"

I kissed her palm, then her lips. "Get some rest, sweetheart. There will be plenty of opportunities for us to help each other out."

Tracy pouted and I couldn't help but smile. "I like helping you out."

"Trust me. I enjoy helping *you* out just as much, if not more," I grunted. "But you need to sleep. We both need to be in good shape to get out of here."

She stared at me, then groaned and rubbed a hand over her face. "Oh my God, I completely forgot where we are!"

"If it's any consolation, until about five minutes ago, so did I," I chuckled. I gently brought her cheek back down to my shoulder and stroked her hair. "Rest," I said again.

"Fine," she sighed. "But if I don't wake up with your dick in me, I'm going to be *very* disappointed."

A laugh burst from my chest. "I'll see what I can do, sweetheart."

"You'd better, daddy."

***

UNFORTUNATELY, NEITHER OF US WAS AWAKENED BY SLEEPY SEX.

My senses were on high-alert now, so even in my sleep, I heard footsteps stop in front of the pool house door before the automatic metal lock scraped open. Therefore, I was able to yank a blanket up over us moments before Owen stepped into the room.

He was, of course, flanked by two guards and I could see four more in the living room through the bedroom door. Not taking any chances, this one.

The bastard opened his mouth to speak, but I pressed a finger to my lips. He smirked, but gestured for me to follow him into the living room. He even stepped out to give the illusion of privacy.

Tracy made a soft sound of protest and reached for me as I eased myself out from under her. I tucked her hand under the pillow I scooted under her head and kissed her temple. "I'll be right back, sweetheart. Get some sleep."

She made another disgruntled sound, but drifted off as I stroked her hair. Then I carefully got up and headed to the closet, pulling on a pair of boxers before walking out into the living room. I closed the door behind me.

"That's just so sweet," he grinned. "Almost as sweet as watching you two do it last night."

I'd known there were cameras. It still didn't make me feel less sickened. "I'm sure you enjoyed yourself," I said, my tone dripping with acid. "Now, what do you want this fine morning?"

"Right now? Her. She's young and takes dick well. I think we could have a lot of fun." He raised his eyebrow in challenge.

"That's never going to happen, asshole," I seethed, crossing my arms over my chest. Despite my bravado, I couldn't help but glance at the closed bedroom door.

"I know. You'd kill the both of you first. But I do like to see you sweat," he chuckled darkly.

"I'm glad you understand." My eyes narrowed on his smirk. "What do you want?"

Owen sat down on the sofa, spreading his arms along the back and crossing one leg over the other. "Why don't you sit down, Nate?"

"I'd rather not," I said.

He nodded to the guards. Two grabbed me and forced me into one of the chairs across from him. "You are so stubborn, Nate. I'm actually rather glad that hasn't changed—makes you more fun to fuck with."

"I'm waiting," I replied, ignoring his jab.

"I have a problem you're going to take care of. Unfortunately, it's going to require you to put on clothes. You look so intimidating with all those muscles," he laughed. "That would be helpful. Maybe an open shirt?"

"Where are we going?" I asked. "I'm not leaving Tracy here with you and your goons."

"Don't worry; I'm going with you," he said. "As for my 'goons,' they know what will happen to them if they touch what is mine." His voice had taken on such darkness that even I felt threatened.

"I'm still not going anywhere without Tracy," I argued.

"Tsk." He looked me up and down. "I suppose I can't be too surprised. You fell for her whore of a mother, too."

"What?" I responded, confused. "What does Lillian have to do with any of this? Do you have her, too?"

Owen guffawed loudly.

"Shh!" I hissed. "She has a concussion. She needs to rest!"

He wiped a tear from the corner of his eye, managing to swallow the rest of his laughter. "Oh, that would be something. I might consider it. We'll call it *Sophie's Choice*. It's not like she's hard to get. Wave a little money in the air and she'll smell it like a bloodhound."

"Look. I don't know what the *fuck* you're talking about, but whatever it is, just leave Lillian out of it. I don't want Tracy worrying about her mother on top of everything else," I said.

"See, and it would almost be boring because you've already made your choice. You just don't know it yet. But I think that, fairly soon, you will understand exactly what the fuck I'm talking about." His smile was disturbing. "I think that's the day I'll crush you."

I just shook my head. "Whatever. What do you need me to do?"

"Put on some clothes. And… wake Tracy up. She can stay in the car. Better yet, you'll do it in front of the car, then she can watch." He rubbed his hands together like some sort of supervillain.

Whatever he wanted, I knew I wasn't going to like it, but at least he'd taken a step back on the Tracy issue. I wasn't leaving her here. No fucking way.

"Give me a minute," I said. The guards let me up and I went back to the bedroom. I closed the door behind me. "Tracy," I whispered, sitting on the edge of the bed. "You have to get up, sweetheart."

She let out a little whine of protest, then sighed and opened her eyes. "Nate?"

"We have to go somewhere with Owen. We need to get dressed." I rubbed her arm. "Let's get you up."

"I don't want to go anywhere with Owen," she grumbled, but sat up just the same.

"I know. I don't, either," I responded. I tugged the blanket down and lifted her out of bed.

Tracy automatically wrapped her arms around my neck. "Where are we going?" she asked as I brought her to the bathroom.

I had my suspicions. In fact, I was certain. "They're taking me to go kill someone."

14

OWEN'S ASSASSIN

Tracy

"WHAT?!!!" I couldn't stop myself from yelling.

Nate shushed me gently. "Don't give him the satisfaction of knowing he's getting under your skin."

"Yes, but... but... it... we... you... how... *Why* are you so calm?" I asked, lowering my voice.

"Because there is nothing I can do about it—and, like I said, I'm not going to give that asshole the satisfaction of seeing me upset," he replied. He set me on my feet and started the shower, keeping me away from the water until he'd decided it was the right temperature. Then he took off his boxers and pulled me in with him.

There was plenty of room in the shower, but I still pressed my wet body to his, laying my head on his shoulder and settling my hand over his heart. "Nate, this is going to kill you."

He kissed the top of my head and cupped water in his palms, soaking my hair. "Probably," he admitted. "But the longer I can do it, the longer he'll let us live, and the longer we live, the more opportunities we'll have to escape."

"But... I mean..." I looked into the bedroom, half expecting to see

Owen lurking there. "What if he wants you to shoot a kid or something?" I whispered.

Nate winced. "Then I'm afraid we won't be getting out of here alive."

"So you won't do it?" I asked hopefully.

"No."

I relaxed into him, relieved. "Good."

He tipped my chin up and kissed me. "I couldn't do it, and I couldn't make you watch that, either."

Bile rose in my throat. "They want me to watch."

"Yes."

Tears of frustration stung my eyes. "I see."

"Oh sweetheart." He framed my face with his hands and kissed my tears away. "I'm going to find a way out of this. I am. I… it was either leave you here with the guards or take you with me. And Owen already—" He suddenly clamped his mouth shut.

"Owen already what?" I asked.

Nate shook his head and began shampooing my hair.

I grabbed his wrists. "Owen already what?"

"I'd rather not say. I don't want to scare you," he mumbled.

"Too late. I'm already scared. What does he want from me?" I responded.

He sighed heavily. "What a man like him typically wants from a woman."

It didn't take long to dawn on me what that was. I nearly threw up. "He wants to have sex with me?"

"He wants to rape you," he replied quietly. His expression turned fierce. "But I won't let that happen, and he knows it."

"How will you stop him?" I felt the first flutters of despair.

Nate looked me right in the eyes. "I will kill us both before that happens."

Strangely, his words triggered a wave of relief rather than fear. "Promise?"

"I swear," he said vehemently.

I nodded and leaned into him again, closing my eyes. He went back to washing my hair. As his fingers massaged my scalp, I melted and gave a little moan. Nate paused. His heart pounded under my palm.

I knew he was hard before I felt his rigid length press against my thigh. With a swallow, he ignored his predicament and began rinsing suds out of my hair.

"Nate?" I said.

"Yes, sweetheart?" he replied.

I rubbed my thigh against his dick. "Please fuck me, daddy."

He drew in a sharp breath, his fingers stopping altogether. "I was really trying to get you clean."

"I'd rather you get me dirty." I reached down and stroked his cock.

One second I was standing in the middle of the shower with him —the next, cool tile hit my back. He didn't prep me at all. I didn't need or want him to. He simply thrust home, crushing his lips against mine.

I cried out and he slanted his mouth over mine, swallowing the sound. He lifted me. "Wrap your legs around me."

I did as I was told, wrapping my legs around his waist. I clung to him as he began drilling me against the shower wall. It was not gentle. My already-sore passage throbbed, but not just with pain. In fact, the more he kept thrusting, the better I felt. "M-more," I begged.

Nate was definitely a breast man. He was so busy pinching and pulling at my nipples that he blinked foggily at me. "Hm?"

I tugged on his hair to get his full attention. "Daddy, I want more."

He chuckled. "Okay, sweetheart. I'll give you more." He shoved himself into me so hard my lower back ground against the tile. He'd never gone that deep before.

"Y-yes, daddy. Oh my God…" I gasped, then groaned when he kept it up—thrusting hard, fast, and deep.

"Who's your daddy?" he rumbled in my ear, nipping the shell.

"Y-you are!" My teeth were chattering. It wasn't going to be long.

Nate nodded, satisfied with my answer. "Come for me, sweetheart."

I came without him even touching my clit. When I would have cried out, he pressed his lips to mine again and captured the sound.

Then he groaned and released his hot cum into me. I trembled with the aftershock of what we'd just done. I panted and laid my head on his shoulder. He laid his head on mine.

"Fuck," he whispered.

"We just did," I pointed out.

"Minx." He pinched my nipple. He'd made them so sensitive by now that I couldn't help but moan.

His dick twitched inside me. "Sonofa—shit. We can't go again now. I've got to wash all that cum out of you from last night and… well… just now. Not put more in."

"Too bad," I lamented. Still, I didn't let go of him.

He made no move to pull out. "We need to get washed and dressed."

"We do," I agreed. "I'll bet that bastard walks right in when he gets impatient."

"He will."

Neither of us moved.

"I really wish we could go again," I sighed.

"Me, too." He kissed me. It was just as tender as his lovemaking had been rough. My insides went all gooey and I rubbed myself against him like a needy cat.

"Ah, fuck it." He started thrusting again.

We both came twice more before he pulled out. I got a fourth orgasm when he washed me clean inside. By that time, he had to prop me up against him because my legs had become jelly.

Nate carried me out of the shower, then patted me dry and wrung out my hair with a towel. I wanted to return the favor, but I was so wobbly, I had to hang onto the counter.

"How are you still standing?" I asked, incredulous, as he toweled himself dry.

"Magic," he grinned.

I snorted. "Uh-huh."

There was a knock at the bedroom door. Nate quickly tucked a towel around me, then wrapped one around his waist, before stepping into the bedroom. "Yes?"

"Are you done screwing in the shower?" Owen's voice came clear through the door. "I would like to get there sometime today."

"We're coming," Nate growled.

"I know that. That's not what I'm asking. I'm asking when you're going to be *finished* coming," Owen laughed.

"Ha-ha." Nate waved me into the bedroom, then pointed to the closet.

I quickly yanked out some clothes and trotted back into the bathroom. There wasn't a door, but at least it gave me some false sense of privacy. I dropped the towel.

The bedroom door burst open.

"For FUCK'S SAKE, Owen!" Nate bellowed as I snatched the towel back up off the floor and held it against my body.

Nate and I both knew he'd gotten his eyeful, however. "Nice," Owen grinned at me. "Tight in all the right places."

I saw Nate raise his fist. "Don't—!"

Four guards tackled him to the floor.

"No! Leave him alone!" I cried, starting forward, no longer caring that I was naked.

Owen held up a hand and the four guards hauled Nate to his feet. "We'll let you get dressed—but don't try my patience. Again." With another motion, the guards let go of Nate and followed Owen out of the bedroom, closing the door behind them.

I dropped the towel, not caring anymore, and ran to Nate. "Nate, are you okay?"

He rubbed his arms, scowling at the closed door. When he turned to me, he had a sweetness in his eyes that made me all gooey inside again. "I'm fine. Let's get dressed."

Those weren't the most romantic sentences uttered by a man, but when he said them with that look on his face, I started feeling... very confusing things. "Good plan," I responded, feeling my cheeks heat up.

His expression softened further. "We'll be together again when we get back, okay sweetheart? Right here on this bed, and every other damn surface in this place."

What the hell am I thinking? I scolded myself. *Of course it's about sex. What else could it be?* I mean, it was what we both wanted, right? A friends-with-benefits sort of situation.

"That sounds nice," I said with more enthusiasm than I felt. Not that I didn't want to fuck on every surface of the pool house—I did and I happily would—it was just... For a moment, it didn't feel like enough. *What the fuck?!* I just stood there, dumbly, more confused than ever.

"Sweetheart?" he asked, his eyebrows drawing together.

I patted his arm. "Sorry. My brain went off the rails for a minute. Let's get dressed before he comes back in."

"I can completely understand going off the rails. This isn't exactly a positive situation we're in here. Plus everything that happened with the FBI and all," he said.

"Right," I agreed. That had to be it. I was just overwhelmed. I went back to the bathroom to retrieve my clothes.

Nate pulled out a suit from the closet. I noticed he didn't button the dress shirt beneath the jacket and didn't bother with a tie.

"I didn't think of you wearing a suit that way," I observed, coming out in my own blouse and dress pants.

"It's not my choice. Owen had an idea about my wardrobe," he grumbled.

"Oh." I walked over and gave him a hug. "Sorry. I didn't mean to rub salt in the wound."

"Not your fault." He hugged me back.

Someone banged on the door. "Hurry up!"

Nate sighed and let me go. He took my hand instead. Giving it an encouraging squeeze, he opened the door. "We're ready."

15

DOING HIS BIDDING

Nate

It was a black Maserati Ghibli Nerissimo with a black interior and red stitching on the leather seats. I knew this because I had one in my garage. I supposed it was Owen's palling-around-town car. Like me, he would have much more expensive models tucked away for special occasions.

Then again, as this model was nearly ten years old, I had a feeling he might have cracked it out just to lord it over me.

"How do you like the car?" he smirked while he chauffeured Tracy and me in the back.

Bingo. "It's almost as nice as mine," I replied.

The corners of his lips turned down in displeasure. "Oh? You have one of these?"

"You know I do," I said.

"Then I'm sure you can see how mine is better." He turned a corner.

I glanced at the SUVs in front of and behind us, then at the bulky guard in the passenger seat not even bothering to conceal the weapon resting on his thigh. Today was not looking good for an escape. "Not really."

"Hm. You'll have to take a closer look when we get there." Owen turned another corner and then suddenly we were driving between stacks of shipping containers.

"Are we there yet?" Tracy asked impatiently, getting in the spirit of the game. I bit back a smile and squeezed her hand. It would be good to find his hot buttons and see what it took to throw him.

"Just about. Why so impatient? Are you that eager to see your lover blow someone else's brains out?" he asked, a malicious grin crossing his face.

"No. I want to get back before lunch. Daddy promised to make me an omelet," she responded in a bored tone.

I covered my startled choke with a sneeze.

Owen's eyebrows hit his hairline as he glanced in the rearview mirror. "*Daddy*?"

"Yes. He promised. Now, would you kindly hurry it up?" She avoided the mirror, not making eye contact with him. Maybe she only trusted her acting skills so far.

"Daddy." He laughed to himself. "I'm going to get you to call me that one of these days."

"Mhm." She examined her fingernails.

"So, Daddy, are you excited for your next assignment?" he asked, his voice still tinged with humor.

"Ecstatic," I muttered. I leaned over and whispered in her ear. "Why did you tell him that?"

She frowned at me. "Tell him what?"

"That I'm your daddy," I said. This close, the strawberry scent of her hair was strong, as well as her matching body wash. Not to mention the intoxicating scent that was uniquely hers. *Fuck.* I wanted this woman bouncing on my dick more than I wanted my next breath.

Her skin flushed as my breath feathered the little baby hairs surrounding her ear. "I thought it might put him off balance or something. I... guess it didn't."

"No. It didn't." My hand moved to her thigh.

Tracy swallowed. "Is-is it important?"

"Not right now," I murmured, staring at her lips.

Owen's loud chuckle brought us back to reality. "Jesus, Daddy, you really are in heat! Don't worry, it should be relatively quick and then we'll get you two back to bed."

Cheeks flaming, Tracy grabbed my hand. I was sure she was going to fling it out of her lap–as she should have. Instead, she paused and threaded her fingers through mine, leaving my hand just five inches from temptation.

My heart pounded. "Tracy—"

"We're here!" he called cheerfully. "Rufus, coordinate with the men and get our special guests ready."

The next thing I knew, our doors were opening and we were being yanked out either side.

"Tracy!" I yelled as she disappeared in a circle of bulky male bodies.

"I'm okay. I'm okay!" she called back, likely suspecting I was on the cusp of doing something stupid.

She wasn't wrong.

Two guards had me by the arms, while another two stood by to prevent said stupid. They turned me to face Owen, who casually stepped out of his car, smirking again.

"What do you want?" I demanded.

"Oh, Daddy. I've told you what I want," he grinned. "I want to see you absolutely destroyed. It might take months. It could take years. But we're going to get there, step by step."

"Great, that's wonderful. What do you want today in particular?" I asked.

He gestured to an open shipping container where a young Latino man was kneeling, trembling.

I got a bad feeling in my stomach. "What did he do?"

"He got sentimental about his sisters being taken by our traffickers, so he followed this container to the United States from Guatemala. Then he released the entire shipment. Fucker." He nodded to one of the two guards on either side of the too-thin, raggedly-clothed man. One of them kicked the man, who buckled onto his hands and knees. It was obvious he'd already been beaten extensively.

My stomach turned. They wanted me to finish him off.

I was so lost in my disgust that it took me a while to realize Rufus was tapping me with the butt of a gun. I stared at it.

Then I looked at Tracy, peeking between her captors. Tears streamed from her eyes, but she nodded.

"No," I finally said quietly.

Owen's eyes lit up. "Really? We've already reached your limit? That's…" He pursed his lips, the excitement going right out of him. "Disappointing."

"I just want to hold her so she isn't scared." I held out my hand toward Tracy. "This has nothing to do with her. Torture me all you want, but make it quick for her."

He waved at his henchmen and they let Tracy go. She ran to me and hit my chest with enough force to almost knock me over. I wrapped my arms around her and buried my face in her hair. "I'm sorry, sweetheart."

"It's okay." She wrapped her arms around my waist. "I knew we weren't going to last long and keep our humanity at the same time. I'm-I'm just glad I got to know you again, Nate."

My throat tightened. "Me, too," I said hoarsely.

"This is sickeningly sweet. But, we all must take our punishment. Now, let's see here…" Owen mused.

I had a very, very bad feeling about what was going to come out of his mouth next.

"You promised you won't let him rape me," she whispered in my ear.

My heart sank, but I knew what she was saying. "I did promise."

"Good. Then we're on the same page." She sounded relieved.

"I think I want her to call *me* daddy," he decided.

Everything in me shattered. Killing her was going to destroy me, but, luckily, one way or another, I wouldn't be alive long afterward. I slowly raised my hands up toward Tracy's throat.

The sound of sirens suddenly filled the air.

"FUCK!!!" Owen looked at Rufus. "Was it you? WAS IT?!!!"

"Sir, I swear—!" Rufus replied, but didn't get a chance to explain as Owen blew a hole through his forehead. The big man slammed to the ground, lifeless, knocking Tracy and me over as well.

I turned so I took the brunt of the fall, then quickly rolled on top of her as the air became alive with gunfire.

"Nathaniel Alton, you *fucking* sonofabitch!" Owen managed to get into one of the two SUVs. He glared death at me as he took off through the containers.

"It's okay," I yelled over the gunfire as Tracy gripped my shirt. Her tears soaked the fabric. "I've got you. I've got you."

When this was all over, I vowed I'd take her to a private island where there was just sun, beach, and quiet. She deserved some quiet after all the shit she was going through. Though, Ecuador wouldn't be bad, either: warm, secluded—we could fuck whenever we wanted...

"Mr. Alton," a familiar voice said, tan boots stopping just beside my head. "Are you going to try to tell me now that you don't know where Tracy Franz is?"

"Agent... Perth?" I asked, looking up. Tracy did, too—her head popped up over my shoulder.

"Good memory." He holstered his sidearm and stared down at us. "I'm getting the distinct impression, Miss Franz, that you're not actually involved in any of your father's operations—or rather, William Masterson Sr.'s. Or, as it turns out, now Owen Jorgensen's. Quite a turn of events, Mr. Alton, that your partner's actually alive."

Said partner was now being dragged back into our little arena, swearing more than a British sailor. "Nate! I am going to fucking *end* you! You motherfucker!"

"How did you find us?" I asked.

Perth made a face. "I had to deal with the worst human I've ever had the misfortune to encounter."

"I thought Masterson was dead?" Tracy said worriedly. "Don't tell me he managed to fake that. Will was so certain..."

"No. Not Masterson—who *is* dead," Perth assured her.

"Who?" Tracy and I asked together.

"Yoo-hoo!" a woman's voice called from a short distance.

All three of us cringed.

"Your mother," Perth answered without needing to.

Lillian Franz-Alton-Alejandro-Mancini-Dale-Richmond walked over to us, as though walking on the clouds of dust being stirred up from the ground. She wore high heels and expensive linen pants—cream-colored and completely inappropriate for her surroundings. She bobbed and weaved through bodies and brain matter with a look of distaste, but they didn't stop her from making her way over to us. "Tracy, dahhhling."

The last time I'd seen Lillian, she would happily have put a stiletto through my eye. Now she smiled at me. "You're so sweet for taking care of her, Nate. I can take over now."

"You told me I was on my own," Tracy said flatly, her fingers digging into my shirt. It was nice to know she was just as against us separating at this point as I was.

"Did I?" Lillian began her gaslighting. "I don't remember that. Maybe you heard me wrong. Anyway, when this nice Mr. Perth here—"

"Agent Perth," Perth sighed and I could tell it was something they'd been going round and round about for a while.

"Whatever." Lillian waved a perfectly lacquered hand. "Come on, dahhhling. Let's go."

Perth cleared his throat. "That's not exactly how this works."

Lillian rolled her eyes. "Ugh. I told you about the stupid network and the stupid silent partner. I even went to *all the trouble* of finding out who it was. If I'm doing your job for you, I expect to be able to take my daughter home with me. And for God's sake, Nate, get off of her! She's practically your daughter."

I didn't much care for Lillian's tone, but I also didn't want to squash Tracy. I began to push myself off her.

To my surprise, Tracy locked her arms around my neck. "Nate, please! Don't leave me with them!"

I wrapped an arm around her back and sat up so she was in my lap. "I won't, sweetheart. I was just getting up."

Lillian's eyes narrowed on me. "Nathaniel Alton, you sonofabitch!"

There were several days in years past that I would have relished in telling this bitch I was screwing her daughter—telling her how much better Tracy was in the sack. But today, I was more concerned about what Tracy thought–how she felt–than I was with pulling one over on her mother. "Mind your business."

"Did you need to compare?" Lillian continued. "Of course I'm better. No one's ever going to suck your dick as good as I did."

"Mother, don't be vulgar. He's not my dad and you're not his wife–you haven't been for years. Plus, I'm twenty-four; I can sleep with whoever I want. I don't need your approval." Tracy said, hugging me tighter.

She was scared they were going to tear us apart. I could tell. I wrapped my arms around her and glared at Perth and Lillian. "Wherever you're taking her, I'll be going."

"That's true," Perth said. "Because *you're* in deep shit, too."

"Tell me something I don't know," I muttered.

16

THE BITCH IS BACK

Tracy

My mother showing up to save my ass was not anywhere on my 'Kidnapping' Bingo card. Hell, if the worst happened, I wasn't sure she'd have shown up to my funeral. I couldn't imagine what she was getting out of helping me; there was no way Lillian Franz did anything if there wasn't something in it for her.

I sat between Lillian and Nate on another jet, ignoring the scathing looks she was giving him—and me. I'd been half afraid he would be all over me, rubbing it in my mother's face, but all he did was hold my hand. Though there was a part of me that would have happily climbed on him to stick it to my mother, I appreciated how much of a gentleman he was.

"You do understand that you two have dug yourselves a hole that's going to be very hard to get out of, right?" Perth asked, coming over and handing out water bottles to the three of us. "Running from the law is never the answer."

Nate frowned at him. "As you can see, we weren't just running from the law."

"You killed three people," Perth persisted. "You wouldn't have been in that situation at all if you'd just let me arrest her."

I looked down at my lap. Perth was right. If I hadn't dragged Nate into this…

Nate rubbed his thumb over the back of my hand. "I'd do it aga—"

"*Must* you fondle my daughter in public?" my mother still seethed.

Nate rolled his eyes. "I seem to remember the tabloids showing you doing a lot more with that Spanish movie star while we were married."

Her grin was malicious. "Jealous?"

"Not for a long, long time," he said in a bored tone.

She pouted then turned her attention to me. "You know, he's not as good as he thinks he is. You should date around some more. Though, I'm sure you've had a broad sampling. You're my daughter, after all."

Heat crept my neck, embarrassment warring with anger in my chest. It was on the tip of my tongue to tell her what I thought of her—and that I was nothing like her, but Nate squeezed my hand.

"Is that really what we're talking about right now?" he grunted. "Agent Perth just might have something important to tell us about–I don't know–prison?"

"Don't be silly. You're not going to prison," my mother scoffed.

Agent Perth raised an eyebrow at her.

"What?" she asked.

"They're definitely going to prison," he said. "At least for some time, while we untangle all this mess."

My mother stiffened. "I don't remember that being part of the deal."

"Deal?" Nate and I echoed together.

"Yes. It seems your mother got herself into a bit of trouble and Count Longfellow decided she wasn't worth the trouble and dropped her. We offered her cash for your whereabouts," Perth elaborated.

"How much?" Nate asked coldly.

"Enough," my mother replied, apple red and fuming.

I, however, was not focused on the money. Rage clawed its way up my throat. "You knew where we were the *whole time* and you weren't going to do anything?!"

Nate's head snapped to look at me, then he glared death at Lillian. "Is that true?"

My mother squirmed in her seat. "I mean… it is an international network."

I slapped my mother, hard, leaving nail tracks on her cheek. "You FUCKING BITCH!!!"

Nate grabbed me and held me tightly, pinning my arms against my chest. "Easy. Easy."

"My face!" my mother wailed, touching her cheek and coming back with beads of blood on her hand.

Perth pulled out a handkerchief and handed it to her.

"We need to get to Switzerland right now," my mother insisted. "I must see my plastic surgeon."

"Why, do you think he'll find your heart?" I sneered, struggling against Nate. "God, you're unbelievable!"

Nate softly kissed the back of my neck. "She's not worth it, sweetheart."

"'*Sweetheart*'? You couldn't come up with something more original?" my mother scoffed. "You called me your lucky star, if I remember correctly, but all you've got for my daughter is 'sweetheart'?"

"Please don't pretend to be concerned about your daughter. You're not that good of an actress," Nate growled.

"I sure fooled you for two years, now didn't I?" my mother replied proudly.

Nate's arms tightened around me, but he didn't show any other sign that she'd gotten to him.

Personally, I'd had enough. "Agent Perth," I said, ignoring her. "How long will we need to stay in prison, do you think?"

"Hard to say," he responded. "I'm hoping not longer than a few months, but it could also be years. It's going to take a lot of hours to untangle everything, plus there's the legal bits that need to be done…"

"You'll look ravishing in orange," Lillian sneered.

"I'm sorry, were you not the center of attention for two seconds? My bad," I shot back.

Nate pulled me into his lap, keeping me out of scratching distance of my mother. "I suppose Lillian gets to wander away with a big bag of money for her help, even though she's obviously close enough to the operation to know where we were."

"Actually," Perth said, "the bag of money gets bigger the more she helps us out. Doesn't it?"

She smiled, giving us both a superior look. "It does. I imagine I will walk out of the FBI headquarters with quite a large bag of money."

"Safe house," Perth corrected. "We need to make sure no one gets to you while you're providing us with information."

I snorted. "Good luck with that."

Perth and my mother frowned at me. Nate understood. "Do you have something to say, *sweetheart?*" she said nastily.

"Just that you're going to die. You're in it now, and frankly, Mother, you don't have the skills it's going to take to make it out the other side alive." I shrugged. "Oh well."

She looked back at Perth. "What is she talking about?"

"I don't know." Perth glared at me. "What are you talking about?"

"I'm talking about the fact that not once—*not once*—have you managed to keep anyone involved with Mastersons that's been in FBI-custody safe. Your 'safe houses' have been useless for safety." I leaned back into Nate, feeling suddenly sad for my mother. "So, if you think it's going to be different with my mother... well... you're delusional. You're also painting a big target on your own back, Agent Perth. I don't know if you're keeping track, but the agents who helped my brother and my friends didn't live long, either."

Lillian stared at me open-mouthed, then rounded on Perth. "Is this true?"

"Look," he replied, shifting uncomfortably. "I won't say things have gone perfectly with this case—"

"It *is* true!" She drew herself up and crossed her arms over her chest. "You could have told me I'd be risking my life by helping you find my daughter!"

"And act as an informant," he reminded her. "Don't forget that part."

"Like hell I will! When we land, I want my money and then I am washing my hands of this whole thing. I'm not sticking my neck out for a few dirty children who don't even matter anyway," she sniffed.

Nate made a sound of distaste and Perth looked disgusted. I wasn't sure what expression was on my face, but I was horrified.

"What?" she asked testily. "It's true. They're probably living even better lives than they would have in their impoverished countries anyway."

Perth rubbed the bridge of his nose. "I'm... not even going to touch this one. I could give you statistics and witness statements, but I have a feeling you wouldn't care regardless."

"I wasn't sure I could think less of you than I already did, Lillian—but I was wrong," Nate muttered.

"Please. You're fucking a girl half your age," she snorted. "Don't act all holier than thou now."

"Mother," I managed after tamping down on my emotions. "You can't possibly mean what you're saying."

"I do," she responded, lifting her chin. "I'm not going to risk my life for a bunch of scraggly refugees. It's none of my business."

I shook my head slowly, staring at her as though seeing her for the first time—maybe I was. "You're a monster."

My mother rolled her eyes. "I don't know where you got that bleeding heart of yours from. It certainly wasn't your father or me. Don't you see? You stuck your neck out and now you're going to prison. You should have left well enough alone; Morgan would have taken care of you and you wouldn't be screwing your grandfather to squeeze a little bit of help out of him. Nate always was a soft touch, but spread your legs for him..."

"Lillian, *shut up!*" Nate snapped.

She gave a triumphant smile. I realized she was proud of getting under his skin.

I squeezed Nate's thigh.

"Temper, temper," she grinned. "Are you getting frustrated in bed? Is it not as good as it was with me?"

"Mother," I began sternly while Nate took my cue and didn't respond.

"We're getting off topic," Perth interrupted. "Ms. Franz…"

"You can just call me Lillian," she said, putting on her best flirty performance.

Perth didn't buy into it. "Ms. Franz. You've made a deal with the United States Government. Unless you want to face the consequences of being linked to the Masterson crime group, I suggest you make good on your end of the deal."

"Are you threatening me?!" she shouted.

"I'm reminding you," Perth replied.

"You can't force me to risk my life!" she exploded. "I won't do it. I won't! You didn't give me all the facts!"

"Welcome to the party," Nate said blandly.

My mother stabbed a finger in Nate's direction. "She roped you in, too!"

"Again, I seem to remember calling you–just once–and you telling me to go twist in the wind…" I interjected. "I didn't rope you into anything. Agent Perth did that."

"Can we please get back to the point?" Perth sighed. "I feel we've wandered into dangerous territory."

"What–not talking about it's going to make it less dangerous? You should have told my mother the truth instead of just flashing green in her face," I argued.

"Hmph. What she said," she agreed.

Guilt suddenly gnawed at my stomach. "I also should have told you the truth," I whispered to Nate while Perth began spluttering excuses.

"You tried," Nate said. He gave my shoulder a brief, soft kiss. "And for the record, I'm glad to be in it with you."

Lillian rolled her eyes. "Honestly, I'm getting a toothache."

"It's… it's a matter of national security. Multiple agencies are involved," Perth finally managed.

"And yet they're still letting the FBI take point. I'm beginning to doubt the intelligence of government Intelligence agencies," Nate said, ignoring my mother.

Perth turned beet red. "We're going to get it right this time."

"Doubt it, but I'll tell you what–if we make it to prison in one piece, I'll give you ten million dollars," Nate replied.

Perth frowned. "Sir, that could be construed as a bribe."

"Just a wager. If it makes you feel better, I'll donate it to the FBI's annual picnic fund," Nate said.

"I don't bet on people's lives," Perth responded stiffly.

"What do you think you're doing right now?" Nate asked.

"My job." Perth gave my mother a sharp look. "You're going to do your duty, ma'am."

"You'll be talking to my lawyer," she shot back.

Angry, Perth shook his head. "I can't wait until we get to headquarters. You three are a real pain in the ass." He stood and walked toward the cockpit.

"We're not going to make it to headquarters," I mumbled. It made me feel tired down to my bones.

"No," Nate agreed. "We're not."

17

NOT GONNA MAKE IT

Nate

Having Tracy in my lap was the only good thing about the entire flight. Perth was sulking at the front of the jet, five other agents spread throughout the cabin, and the pilot. And, of course, Tracy and me–and Lillian.

God, take me now.

"Do you think the FBI will pay my attorney's fees?" Lillian asked as the jet descended to the runway. "They haven't paid me yet and—"

"You're between gold-digging gigs?" I said sweetly.

She scowled at me. "What do you think *she* is?" She nodded at the sleeping Tracy.

"Desperate. And innocent. She doesn't deserve any of this." I absently stroked Tracy's back.

"Don't get too attached. She's a smart girl. She'll leave you when a better opportunity comes along." Lillian gave me a catty smile.

"I very much doubt that." I kept stroking Tracy's back, hoping she'd sleep as long as possible.

"So, what is your arrangement?" Lillian asked. "I mean, just how many times has she screwed you and how many are left?"

My eyes narrowed. "Your daughter is right. You're very vulgar."

123

"You're a businessman above all else, Nate," she continued. "Remember, I know you. So, what kind of deal do you have going on? Is she finally going to give you that heir you wanted?"

"I don't recall telling you I wanted *you* to give me any children. Your kid was already grown up," I replied.

"That doesn't answer my question," she said.

I ground my teeth. "Our relationship–business or otherwise–has nothing to do with you, Lillian. I owe you nothing–and don't even pretend to be a doting mother at this point. You've already proven that you're not."

She gave me a pout that had worked a hundred percent of the time when we were married. Now it was just annoying. "Please, Nate-y-boo? I'm just asking a simple question."

"And I'm going to tell you again that it's none of your business," I responded, feeling a shiver of revulsion at her old pet name for me.

"I'll bet it's more than fifty fucks," she winked.

Tracy stirred and all I wanted to do was cover her ears to stop her from hearing the filth her mother was spewing. "Lillian, I swear to Jesus..."

"I remember when you used to find religion in bed with me." She put her hand on my knee.

I swatted it away. "Do you mind? Your daughter is sleeping."

Lillian pouted again. "You're no fun."

"Okay, folks. We're landing in ten minutes. We'll be in a police-escorted motorcade all the way to FBI headquarters. No mistakes this time," Perth said, coming back from the cockpit.

Tracy yawned, still looking completely wrecked even after hours of sleep. "Still not going to make it."

"You're entitled to your opinion, but the fact is: within the next twenty-four hours, you're going to be in prison awaiting trial," Perth replied.

"We'll see," I added.

Perth grumbled under his breath and took his seat again as we landed. The wheels touched down with a calm little bump. It was a deceptively smooth landing.

"I don't know *what* you were so worried about," Lillian sniffed, as the FBI agents began to mobilize and the door opened.

"That's the advantage of using a private airstrip," Perth said proudly. "We're going to—where's our escort?"

"Ah, fuck," I muttered.

Tracy sighed. "Three... two..."

There was a loud thud and a canister rolled between Perth's feet and into the aisle.

"Flashbang!" Perth and I said at the same time.

I rolled Tracy to the floor, covering her eyes as the flashbang exploded.

Lillian screamed.

"Nate..." Tracy whispered.

"It's okay. Just stay down." I kissed the back of her neck. I opened my eyes to see Perth and the other agents with their guns out, covering the door.

"Close the door and get us the fuck out of here, you idiots!" I yelled.

"Mike! The door!" Perth called to the cockpit.

There was no response.

"MIKE!!!" Perth repeated.

I looked down the aisle and into the cockpit. A hand draped over the side of the pilot's chair and dripped blood that was slowly pooling on the floor. *Figures.* "I think he's dead."

"What?!" Perth sprung up and ran to the cockpit.

"Perth!" I shouted.

There was a soft thud, then he grunted and held his side.

"Perth, you dumb fuck, get out of there! Don't you see your friend Mike was shot?!" I yelled.

"Someone's got to close the goddamn door!" he grunted back.

Boiling inside, I leaned down by Tracy and gently brushed back her hair. "Stay here. Stay down. I'll be right back." When I went to shuffle off her, she grabbed my wrist.

"Please don't go. Don't get hurt," she begged.

I kissed her forehead. "I just have to go help for a minute. I'll be okay." I still ended up having to pry myself loose from her grip.

"Just let him go. Men are all stupid. I'll introduce you to a nice bungee-jumping baron and if we're really lucky, he'll die in one of his extreme sports escapades and leave us his fortune," Lillian said as I passed her, keeping my head below the windows as I made my way down the aisle.

"Missed you, too, Lillian," I muttered.

She gave me her sweetest smile. "Run along and get killed now. The sooner you do, the sooner I can get her through her heartbreak and help her realize that no man is worth it."

There were many things I wanted to say in return, but... *What is it the kids say? 'Don't feed the trolls'?*

Perth was ducked down beneath the control panel by the time I got there, wheezing and holding his side.

"Not sure which button to push?" I asked.

He nodded. "I don't know which one retracts the door."

I studied the control panel from a low position, then pressed what I discerned must be the correct button. The door began to retract.

"Thank God," Perth sighed, slumping against the pilot's lifeless leg.

"Perth." I frowned as his eyes closed.

He didn't answer.

"Perth!" I grabbed his shirtfront and gave him a shake. "Wake up, man!"

He groaned, his eyes unfocused as he blinked them open.

"Who can fly this thing?" I asked. "We need to get airborne."

"Mike..." he mumbled, closing his eyes again.

Fuck that. "Perth!" I shook him harder. "Mike is dead. Who else can fly this bird?"

"N-no one." He coughed up blood. It dribbled down his chin and onto his shirt. "Just Mike." He coughed again.

"Sonofabitch. Why did we bother with the goddamn door if no one can fly the goddamn plane!" I laid him on the floor. "Don't die on me. I can't properly tell you 'I told you so' in this state." I pushed aside his jacket and ripped the hole in his shirt wider so I could see his wound. I didn't like the look of it. It was big and deep and oozing blood. I was sure if the bullet weren't still inside, his blood would be flowing out like a river onto the floor.

Although I could hear a scuffle in the main cabin, at this point, I knew I'd have to let the other FBI agents handle it, or our one ally in the FBI was going to die. I took off my shirt and wadded it up, pressing it hard against the wound. "Hang in there, Perth. I'm sure —"

"What are you sure about, Nathaniel?" a voice asked behind me.

Please don't be Owen. Please don't be Owen... I turned slowly. "Morgan?" I stared at Tracy's father. *What is this, a family reunion?*

"Excuse me a moment, if you will, Nathaniel." Morgan raised a Glock. "I thought we'd taken care of this situation, but you of all people would know that some men just don't know when to lay down and die."

"Morgan, don't," I tried to forestall him. "He just needs medical attention. He's a high-ranking FBI agent. He could still be useful to you."

Morgan laughed. "Your sympathy for a man who was going to put my daughter in prison is adorable, but I'm afraid I can't abide being crossed that way."

Before I could so much as twitch, he'd shot Perth in the head. "Shit." I looked past Morgan, desperately hoping Tracy hadn't seen it happen.

Her wide eyes met mine. I could tell she was bravely fighting back tears. "Fuck, Morgan, your daughter is going to need so much therapy."

"I thought she was getting that from you," Morgan grinned. He pointed his gun at me. "I think you know how this goes."

"Dad, no!" Tracy shrieked, dragging herself up off the floor and starting for the cockpit.

Lillian caught her leg, causing her to trip and fall. "It's for the best. Trust your father."

Tracy knocked her head on the floor and groaned.

"She has a fucking concussion you fucking cunts!" I yelled,

smacking Morgan's gun aside. I really didn't give a damn if he shot me in the back at this point–all I saw was Tracy.

"That really wasn't the best move, love," Morgan *tsked* at Lillian.

Lillian pouted, then sulked as I knelt next to Tracy. "Morgan-bear, I didn't mean to hurt her."

"I know you didn't, Lilly-Lou. We just have to be a bit careful with her right now, that's all," he cooed back.

"Tracy, sweetheart, are you okay?" I asked, ignoring them as I carefully eased her onto her back and framed her face with my hands. "Look at me." She looked up at me with her brilliant ocean eyes and relief washed over me.

"Hi sweetheart," I said softly.

Tracy put her hands over mine. "Nate?"

"Hm? Yes, it's me," I replied.

"Why are my parents not fighting, and calling each other pet names?" She frowned.

Excellent question... When I'd married Lillian, the two of them couldn't stand each other. I was just as surprised as Tracy to see that the situation had changed; I could only stare at the two of them while Lillian made kissy faces at Morgan, and Morgan blew her a kiss.

"Jealous?" Lillian asked after a while.

The very idea made me recoil and Morgan chuckled. "You really did a number on him, Lilly-Lou."

"I'm good at that," she responded proudly.

"You sure are." Morgan said it with equal pride.

"You two never fell out of love," Tracy accused them, trying to sit up. I helped her, then put an arm around her while she scowled at her parents. "You were doing something for that awful Masterson."

"Let's not forget Mr. Jorgensen. He's the one who approached us in the first place. I mean, first he needed help fleecing Nathaniel, but then we realized Lillian is so good at what she does, the opportunities are endless," Morgan explained.

Rage seared my insides as I looked at the two of them. "All those other men..."

"They all had something we needed. Not money, necessarily. In fact, not even usually. The hardest part was having to pretend we hated each other," Lillian shrugged.

"You pretended—even to me?" Tracy asked. "Why?"

"Oh, darling. You were always so terribly moral. I don't know where you got it from. Certainly not us," Lillian sighed.

"No. Certainly not," I grunted.

Morgan lifted his gun again.

"No!" Tracy began climbing into my lap while I pushed her away, trying to put as much distance between her and my bullet as possible. The grappling was probably comical to watch.

Lillian giggled and Morgan snorted. "Relax. I'm just holstering it. Jesus, you'd think we shoot just anybody." He put it in the holster under his jacket.

"And Owen wants you alive," Lillian added.

"And we have plans of our own," Morgan said.

Tracy managed to get into my lap while I eyed her parents with suspicion. She wrapped herself around me and I automatically wrapped my arms around her. "What plans?"

"I'm glad you asked, Nathaniel. You're getting married," Morgan replied.

For some reason, that made me clutch Tracy tighter. "The hell I am."

"To our daughter," Lillian elaborated.

18

WEDDING BELLS

Tracy

"I'm sorry, what did you just say?" Nate asked.

I felt the strangest leap of excitement inside me. *What was that all about?!* I should have felt anger, revulsion, something more appropriate. But I didn't.

"You heard us," Dad said. "Our daughter seems as disinclined as you are to contribute to the family business, so we've decided, as good parents, we need to set her up somewhere she can thrive, but also not be a nuisance. She went to you on her own, which gave us the idea. Obviously if she's letting you fuck her, she's not repulsed by you–and clearly Owen can easily keep you both on a very short leash. It's win-win all around. I mean, you liked Lillian just fine. Now you get to park your Ferrari in the younger version's garage. What's not to like?"

"You're disgusting," Nate replied as he rubbed the back of my neck. He had that nice way of trying to comfort me, even if he wasn't aware of it. "You shouldn't talk about your daughter like she's an asset, or hell, a piece of steak."

I turned to scowl at my parents. "That's right. That's gross."

"Darling, you are an asset," Mother said. "We'd hoped you'd be a much more..." She gestured vaguely.

"Valuable asset," Dad provided.

"Thank you, Morgan-bear. A much more valuable asset. But I have no idea how it happened—you inherited your brother's moral fiber. I thought that came entirely from Will Jr., but apparently some part of me has bad genes." She pouted at my father. "I'm sorry, Morgan-bear. It must be completely my fault."

"Aw, no, Lilly-Lou. Don't say that. I have some family a generation back who became… doctors and surgeons. One even renounced her inheritance and became a… a *social worker*." My father sounded sickened by the very idea.

"What's wrong with helping people?" I asked.

My mother took one of my hands. It made my skin crawl. "There's nothing wrong with it, darling. It's just not what we do. We have to protect our wealth, you see. If you're not growing it, well, you might as well flush it right down the toilet. Nate understands."

"Nate doesn't traffic children," I said, pulling my hand away.

"Nate sure did when he didn't know what his partner was doing," Dad chuckled.

Nate's whole body stiffened and I turned back quickly and hugged him. "It wasn't your fault. Don't even think that."

He burrowed his face in my hair. "Maybe if I'd paid attention…" he whispered.

"It wouldn't have helped. You'd be dead or worse," Mother said. "There's no use crying over spilled milk. Now, should we continue this conversation in the limo?"

Dad chuckled. "How did you know I brought a limo?"

"Because my Morgan-bear would never let me ride in anything less." Mother made kissy faces at Dad again; he did it right back.

Nate carefully stood while I was still wrapped around him. "Just hang on, sweetheart. I'll get you to the car."

"Li-mo," Mother enunciated. "My Morgan-bear would never bring just some old car."

"Whatever." Nate brushed past her and Dad.

"Careful on the stairs," Dad called after us.

Nate paused at the top of the stairs and I wondered why. Then I saw five bound FBI agents on the hangar floor.

"Are they alive?" I asked.

"Yes."

I took a shuddering breath before my next question. "Will they be for long?"

I could feel him swallow. "No."

I buried my face in his neck. "God."

"Keep your eyes closed." His hand rubbed up and down my back. "Just… don't look."

"Are you stuck?" Dad asked behind us.

"Just taking some precautions," Nate replied. I clung to him, face pressed into his skin so I couldn't see even if I wanted to, as he started down the stairs.

"Oh. You mean this business." Dad was completely dismissive. "They should have been dispatched by now." He snapped his fingers.

Nate's hand pressed hard into the back of my head. "Don't look."

I didn't. I heard several loud bangs, but I kept my eyes shut. The horror of it made me shudder, even without actually seeing it.

"Ugh. Morgan-bear, that's so gross," Mother complained.

"Yes, but necessary, my love," Dad said.

Nate didn't put me down until we got to the limo, and even then, he blocked my view with his body as I got inside. He sat down next to me and took my hand, putting his other gently over my eyes. "It's just about done."

"Okay." I squeezed his hand with both of mine.

"Ugh. California is so hot this time of year," Mother lamented as she got into the limo.

"We'll be back in Minnesota soon enough. How are you doing with the wedding arrangements, Lilly-Lou?" Dad asked. The car door shut and he tapped what I assumed was the partition. "Oscar. To the beach house."

The limo started to move and, after a minute or two, Nate took his hand away from my eyes.

"It's all arranged for a month from now. You wouldn't *believe* how difficult it is to put on something decent with only a week to prepare," Mother sighed.

"We're not getting married." Nate emphasized each word, tapping his finger against his knee. "Tracy is too young to be thinking about that, especially with me."

"Why not with you?" I blurted before my parents could respond.

Nate raised his eyebrows in surprise. "I'm old enough to be your father."

"That hasn't stopped us from doing other things." I wished I could stop my mouth, but apparently I had things to say.

"Yes… but that's different," he said.

I wanted to know how it was different, but I finally managed to make myself shut up. I turned and stared out the window.

"Tracy, sweetheart…" he murmured, touching my shoulder.

"I just need a minute," I said softly.

Nate removed his hand. "Okay."

Unfortunately, my parents were still there–something I should have taken into account before opening my big mouth.

"I know they say you shouldn't buy the cow when you can get the milk for free, but in this case, Nate, you're going to have to buy the cow, I'm afraid," Dad chimed in.

My stomach turned in disgust.

"Did you just call your daughter a cow?" Nate growled.

"Aw, Nate-y-boo, don't get so riled up." Mother patted his knee.

Nate slapped her hand away. "Lillian, touch me one more time and I swear…"

She cupped her hand to her chest. "Ow."

Dad turned almost purple with rage. "Did you just slap my wife?"

"I did. Do you have a problem with that?" Nate shot back.

Dad looked as though he was going to go for his gun, but then crossed his arms over his chest instead. "Hm. I suppose we could ask Owen if he's in the market for a lightly-used wife."

My blood ran cold. "No, Dad!"

"He'd probably be able to convince her to get on board with the operation," Dad continued. "Yes. Why didn't we think of it before?"

"You're so smart, Morgan-bear," Lillian simpered. She cuddled into his side and eyed me in a speculative way that made me very, very frightened. "I think it would be easy to exchange one groom for another."

I looked up at Nate, wondering what he was thinking.

He was pale. His fingers were digging into his thighs. "Don't," he said.

"Don't? Don't what?" Mother asked, smirking.

"Don't give Tracy to Owen. I'll do it. I'll marry her," he replied in defeat.

"I thought you might change your mind." My mother looked up at Morgan. "But it would probably be a better match and make Tracy useful one day."

"True," Morgan said, rubbing his chin.

Nate trembled imperceptibly; I could feel his vibration where our thighs touched. "What do you want?" he asked the scheming pair.

"Now we're getting there," Mother responded. "But how can a mother possibly put a dollar amount on her daughter?"

"I can." Morgan used his finger and pretended to count in the air. "Let's see here, carry the one…"

"Stop." I took Nate's hand, threading my fingers through his.

"Stop what?" Dad asked innocently.

"Just stop. STOP. Can't you please try to remember I'm your daughter?" My eyes stung, but I viciously forced myself not to cry. "I'm not a cow, or an asset, or anything like that. I'm your *daughter*. Doesn't that matter to you at all?"

Lillian bit her lip, putting a hand on Morgan's shoulder. "Of course it matters, darling. We were just having some fun."

"It isn't fun for me," I said.

"Tracy, you were always going to marry Nate–from the moment you went to him for help. Owen was going to play with you for a while, but ultimately–once he got Nate roped in–you were going to be married and returned to Minnesota," Dad explained.

"I'm fairly certain Owen intended to kill us," Nate argued.

"Well, he doesn't intend to now," Mother said. "Though I'm sure he'll be happy to hear about the death of Agent Perth."

Nate shook his head slowly. "Perth was a good man."

"He was a moron," my father scoffed. "Going up against our organization with a handful of agents–what did he think was going to happen?"

"Is… Owen free already?" I asked.

"I'm sure he is, sweetheart," Nate sighed.

Morgan smiled. "Of course he is. It turns out it was all a big misunderstanding."

"Of course it was," Nate muttered.

"Don't be so bitter, Nate-y-boo. You get to marry our darling little angel and have a whole mansion full of kids," Mother beamed.

"Why do you keep bringing up kids?" Nate asked. "Tracy has a lot of time for that, and—"

"Your journal was fascinating reading, Nate-y-boo," Lillian said.

"It was," Morgan agreed, grinning from ear to ear. "Sad you never had any family."

Nate drew a sharp breath but didn't rise to the bait.

"So cute that you want to make one of your own," my snarky mother added.

"Stop it! Both of you!" I yelled at my parents. Nate's hand tightened in mine. "You're both awful! Why would you do that to Nate? I mean, after everything *you've* done–invading his privacy that way?!"

"I mean, we read yours, too," my dad confessed.

My jaw dropped. "You *what*?!"

"How else are we supposed to keep tabs on you?" Lillian asked.

"I find it adorable that we're forcing you to marry Nate; you already find what we do reprehensible; and yet, reading your diaries is the breaking point," Morgan laughed.

It *was* a strange place to draw the line, I'd be the first to admit it. But something in me snapped. "I hate you both."

The bastards actually laughed! "Oh, darling, we know. You're going to resent us for the rest of your life," Lillian said.

"But you're finally going to fall in line," my father added. "And that's what matters."

"I *am* just an asset to you," I accused them.

"Finally, a glimmer of understanding," Morgan said. "I was afraid you were never going to get there."

I tried so hard to keep the tears inside, but I felt a traitorous one slip down my cheek.

"Darling, don't be so upset. We're marrying you to a man that *even you* consider 'good'. You have good chemistry. You're set. All you need to do from now on is lay back and take dick and pop out babies," my mother smiled.

"Still vulgar, Lillian," Nate interjected, grinding his teeth.

She shrugged. "It's the truth."

"Here we are," Morgan announced.

I looked out the window as the limo pulled up to a wisteria-covered house with a terracotta roof. *House* was a bit of an under-statement, of course, but it was smaller than our mansion back in Minnesota.

"Isn't it lovely? You'll be staying here for a while. You're going to have a beach ceremony behind the house in a month. We're going to tell everyone it was a whirlwind romance." Lillian proudly laid out the plan for us.

"Of course, everyone is going to wonder if Nate spite-fucked the younger model and Tracy got pregnant, but that can't be helped," Morgan said.

To our credit, Nate and I did not react–or so I thought….

"You both turned a little pink. There was actual spite-fucking, wasn't there?" Morgan chortled.

Nate opened the car door just before Oscar got to it. "If you'll excuse us, Tracy and I are tired. I think we'll just get settled in." He slid out, tugging me out behind him.

"You two have a nice 'rest,'" Lillian giggled. "We'll be staying at the next property over."

"I'm sure you know the drill–guards, cameras, and all that." He gestured toward the entire building. "Don't bother trying to escape."

"Wouldn't dream of it," Nate said.

19

———

NEW DREAMS

Nate

When we got into the house, with the door securely closed behind us, I pulled Tracy against me. "Cry, sweetheart. Cry."

She buried her face in my shirt and let out a sob.

"There we go. Keep going," I whispered in her ear, rubbing the back of her neck, my other arm around her waist, holding her tight to me.

Then she screamed into my shirt. "I can't believe those are my parents!"

"I know, sweetheart. I know. They're terrible people." I kissed her hair and rocked her gently, my heart breaking for her. "Let's just say they're not your parents, all right? I know it's impossible that monsters like them created someone as perfect as you."

"Well, they did," she mumbled.

I tipped her chin up. I was just going to talk to her, but her wounded ocean eyes made me groan and lose all restraint. I kissed her. She didn't pull away; in fact, she pressed closer.

With a groan, I backed her up against the foyer wall. Every terrible thing that had built up inside me needed an outlet. My body and mind decided it was going to be her.

139

She had the same idea, desperately rubbing against me. "Nate…"

"I know, sweetheart. I'm not going to stop," I murmured, working a hand between us and palming her breast through her shirt.

I'd had no intention of stopping, anyway. However, someone delicately cleared their throat.

"Fuck," I swore, dragging my lips from Tracy's. I glared at the slight, middle-aged woman with her hair pulled back in a neat French braid. "Can I help you?"

Tracy dropped her forehead onto my shoulder and panted. My hand was still on her breast. I wasn't moving it if I didn't have to.

"I'm sorry, Mr. Alton. I was asked to give you a tour of the house and grounds," the woman said stiffly. "My name is Marina, and—"

"I'm only interested in knowing where one place is right now. Where is our bedroom?" I asked.

"Oh good. I'm glad you didn't assume you'd have separate rooms," Marina replied. "I will also show you the—"

"BED-ROOM," I insisted. "Anything else can wait."

Marina pursed her lips. "Alright, sir. This way."

Tracy was shaking in my arms. I looked back, concerned, only to see that she was trying not to laugh.

"You'll thank me in a minute," I said. Reluctantly, I took my hand off of her breast and laced my fingers through hers, turning to follow Marina.

"You're… um… hard, Nate," Tracy whispered to me as Marina led us up a winding staircase and down a long hallway.

"And I'm going to be until a certain goddess puts me out of my misery," I replied. "I don't give a damn what anyone on this property thinks–except you."

She blushed. "I will, you know."

"You will what?" I asked.

"I'll… um… put you out of your misery."

I rubbed my thumb against her palm. "I know, sweetheart. We both need this."

Marina finally brought us to a bright, airy bedroom with Spanish decor and a California King bed. "Now," she said, gesturing around, "as you can see—"

"Thank you, Marina. That will be all for today," I said loudly, dropping Tracy's hand only so I could steer Marina out the door.

"Wait! Sir! Dinner is at—" Marina began.

"Dinner is on a tray outside this door or dinner isn't happening," I cut her off. "*THANK YOU*, Marina. *THAT WILL BE ALL.*"

Her expression screamed disapproval, but she was too good of a housekeeper to *say* what she was thinking. "Very good, sir. Dinner will be on a tray outside the door in an hour. Please understand it will get cold even with the cloches."

"Good to know. Have a lovely evening." I slammed the door in her face.

Tracy had a hand over her mouth and was shaking with suppressed laughter. "Poor Marina!"

"She'll get over it." I pulled her against me and she gasped. "I think we left off here?" I pressed my lips to hers and possessively palmed her breast.

"Uh-uh-huh," she responded, shivering as I thumbed her nipple through her shirt. I moved down to her neck, kissing her there, too. At that moment, I remembered Lillian and Morgan talking about marrying her off to Owen, and my blood boiled.

"Sweetheart." I tried not to growl. "I need to do something."

"What?" she asked. When I looked up, her cheeks were flushed and her eyes slightly glazed. She blinked a few times. "You sound a little scary. Are you going to go kill someone?"

Not a drop of horror in her tone, just acceptance. Fuck, this woman was *made* for me. "Not right now. I just..." I kissed her delicate skin, then grazed my teeth over the spot. "I need to mark you."

"*Mark* me?" She looked a bit less dazed, but very confused. "Like a hickey?"

"Yes. It will bruise and be visible unless you wear a turtleneck, but... I don't want anyone else thinking they can touch you. You're mine," I said.

She combed her fingers through my hair, giving me a look so soft that it made me ten times more desperate to have her. "Like Owen?"

"Exactly like Owen," I seethed.

"Oh." She bit her lip. "You're asking if you can do that now or while we're having sex?"

"During sex. I don't want to just go and bite you. I'd do it while I was making you feel good. I just don't want to be the kind of man who leaves deliberate marks on your body without asking first," I replied. "And we won't both be clear-headed during. We're barely clear-headed now."

"True." She trailed her fingertips down my chest.

It was only then I remembered I'd sacrificed my shirt to try to save Perth. Goosebumps rose on my bare skin. "Sweetheart?"

"It's okay, daddy," she said, bending to lick my nipple.

I thought my dick was going to explode. "It's okay?" I wheezed.

"It's okay," she repeated. "You can mark me; I am yours, so why not? I don't mind who sees."

My heart pounded and dangerous thoughts filled my head. Thoughts I should not have been having about a twenty-four-year-old. But I couldn't stop myself; I wanted more than her body. I wanted to be more than friends with benefits; I wanted to be a significant part of her life. God help me, when Lillian and Morgan began talking about marrying Tracy to me, I'd started having visions of her in white coming toward me on the beach. I knew exactly how she'd look; how she'd smile; how her hair would tickle my cheek in the breeze when she finally stood beside me...

"Nate?" she asked. "Did you hear me?"

I shook myself, banishing the thoughts to the back of my mind. "Yes, sweetheart. I heard you. I just got caught up in my own little world, that's all."

Tracy gave me a fake pout. "What, with all this in front of you?" She gestured to herself—rumpled clothes, flushed cheeks, mussed hair and all.

"You make an excellent point." I hooked my fingers in the waistband of her shirt and pulled it up past her bra.

She smiled and raised her arms. I stripped it right off her. I backed her to the bed and sat her down on the edge, kneeling in front of her. Then I molded her breasts between my hands, the perfect globes swelling over the top of her bra. "Hello girls. Daddy's home."

Tracy gave a shriek of laughter. "Daddy, you're crazy."

"Crazy about you," I said without a thought. I pillowed my face in her breasts as I reached behind her back to snap her bra open.

"You know, the bra's not going to come off if your face is there," she chuckled, tugging on my hair.

"Mm. Five more minutes," I faked a whine.

Her giggles were the most beautiful sound I'd ever heard. I tipped my face up from her cleavage and saw her looking at me with…

… the most *loving*…

Ah, hell. We'd need to talk about this later, but right now, we were both too far gone.

She slipped the bra off while I was distracted and dangled it from one finger. "Missing this?"

Considering the large, pert, perfect feat I now had before me? "Not really," I said, taking a nipple into my mouth. "Sweetheart, you're so tasty…"

"Like hard candy, right daddy?" she gasped, cradling my head as I played with her breasts.

"You were listening," I grinned. I slid my hand under her skirt and up the inside of her thigh. The little minx toed off a shoe and rubbed the ball of her foot against my cock. I nearly lost it right there in my pants. With a grunt, I grabbed her ankle. "Sweetheart…" I warned her.

Tracy leaned forward and kissed me, then breathed in my ear, "I want you, daddy."

Whatever slow seduction I'd had planned flew right out the window. I stood and pushed her back on the bed. "Skirt. Off." She nodded, panting slightly as she reached behind her hips for the zipper.

I might have set a world record in the brief time it took to shed my pants and boxers. My dick was already dripping precum. I looked back up to see Tracy still struggling with her skirt.

"It's caught on the lace. My panties," she said, frustrated. She wriggled on the bed, rolling from one side to the other.

Fuuuuuuck. If I wasn't inside this woman soon, I was going to have an aneurism. "How much do you like that skirt and panties?" I growled.

"I mean, they're not even mine—" she began.

I loomed over her, grabbed both edges of the back of the skirt from her hands, and ripped it all the way down the back. The panties, of course, decided they needed to be ruined as well.

I didn't give a fuck. The way she grabbed them from me and kicked them the rest of the way off told me she didn't, either.

"Fuck me, daddy," she begged, spreading her legs. "Please. I need you so badly."

Holding back was painful. "You're not warmed up enough yet."

She grasped my hand and placed it between her legs. "Then warm me up."

2 0

WARM ME UP

Tracy

Nate was losing his mind. I could see the way his cock was leaking, and there was a primal look in his eyes. I couldn't believe he had the restraint to make sure my body was ready for him.

I didn't.

"Daddy…" I whined as he moved his fingers inside me. "Please…"

"Just about there, sweetheart," he replied with effort.

I held onto his wrist and ground against his hand. It felt good, but I knew he could give me something bigger and better–more importantly, I needed to feel that connection. "Daddy…"

He gave a heavy sigh. "You don't make it easy on an old man."

"You're not an old man," I insisted.

"Hm." He didn't sound convinced.

"You're n—" I gasped when he removed his fingers. "Nate?"

He slowly licked each finger one by one. "I think we're ready, sweetheart."

Relief mixed with the burning hot desire within me. "Good."

"Good what?" he asked, lifting my hips a little and lining himself up.

My mouth watered. "Good, daddy."

"Better. And what do you want daddy to do?" He pushed gently, the tip of him sliding inside me.

I whimpered with need.

Nate pinched my nipple. "Come on, sweetheart. You have to tell daddy what you want."

"P-please," I said, moving my hips, trying to take in more of him.

"Please what?" he teased, not helping me one bit.

"Please fuck me, daddy!" I cried.

He thrust hard, burying his cock inside me. While I let out a shout of satisfaction, he pressed his forehead to mine. "That's my good girl," he murmured. "God, you feel fantastic."

"Y-you, too," I managed, wrapping my arms around him. His back was tense, just like the rest of him, as he moved inside me–he was holding back. "Daddy, you can go harder."

"Mm-mm. Concussion," he reminded me, his voice strained.

Oh right. I bit my lip. "It doesn't hurt and I'm not dizzy."

"That's wonderful, but you're not going to change my mind," he replied.

"But—"

Nate nipped my shoulder. "Listen to daddy."

I gaped. "Hey!"

"We're not going to risk your health any more than we already are," he admonished me. "If I wasn't a heartless bastard who can't keep his hands off you, we wouldn't have gone this far, either." He nuzzled my breast. "God help me, Tracy."

I tugged on his hair so he would look at me. "I need this, too, you know."

"I know." He pressed his lips to mine and switched it up with a sinful swivel of his hips.

My toes curled and I felt delicious tingles all through my body, but I wasn't letting him off that easily. I pulled his hair again. "I mean it, I —ah!—I—oh God... Nate you aren't playing fair!"

He groaned and pulled my hands from his hair, kissing my fingers before trapping them above my head with one big hand. "All's fair in love and war," he mumbled, his hips grinding against mine as he thrusted. His eyes were fixed on my bouncing breasts; if he wasn't using his other hand for leverage, I was sure he'd be paying them homage right then.

I was equally sure he wasn't aware of the words that had just dropped from his mouth–but I was. I nearly stopped breathing. "What?"

"Shh, let daddy take care of you," he said, thrusting with a little more force. It was what I'd wanted the whole time, but suddenly not the point anymore.

I arched my back and cried out, my inner muscles clamping down on his cock as my first orgasm overtook me.

With my eyes squeezed shut, I didn't know what was happening until I felt a sting on my neck at the height of my pleasure. It startled me, but also made me have a second orgasm on the heels of my first.

Nate chuckled as he released his warm cum into me, letting go of my hands and wrapping his arms around me. He licked the spot and I shivered, for some reason feeling the sting in my nipples and all the way down to where we were joined.

"You liked that, didn't you, sweetheart?" He rolled onto his back so I was sprawled on top of him, my legs splayed wide and my body happily holding his dick inside.

I could also feel that his dick was happy to be there. "You're still hard. Again."

"Is that a complaint?" he teased. "If so, I'm afraid you'll have to take it up with customer service—"

"As if I'd ever complain about that," I snorted. I smoothed my hand over his chest, playing with the salt-and-pepper chest hair there, trying to gather up the courage to ask my next question. "Why did you say 'all's fair in love and war'?"

He tensed, his fingers stilling in my hair. "What?"

"You heard me." I leaned up so I could look him in the eye.

Nate raked a hand through his hair. "It's just... you know... a saying. I'm sure I was making a joke."

"You were."

"Then why so serious? It's just a joke," he said. He sounded very sure of himself.

I nodded. "Okay." I hadn't known how I'd feel either way, but now I was… strangely disappointed. I laid back down, suppressing a sigh. My eyes stung, but I wouldn't let myself cry. It was too soon, too sudden. He had a hang-up about our age gap and probably a zillion other reasons not to be with me long-term. I understood. Okay, I was *trying* to.

His fingers grazed down my spine as we laid there quietly. He made no move to initiate sex again, but he also didn't pull out.

"Tracy?" he finally asked.

"Mhm?" I replied, still not quite trusting myself to speak.

"Do you… want it to not be a joke?" he continued carefully.

I took a shaking breath, hating myself for how emotional I was when he was so calm. "You don't want to know my answer."

"I do," he argued.

"You'll try to talk me out of it," I said with a hard swallow.

"I imagine I will," he said. "Many times."

I leaned up again and gave him a hard look. "You'll lose."

"Oh, of that I am absolutely certain," he murmured. His rough fingers wiped gently under my eyes and I realized I was crying.

"Shit," I muttered, pushing his hand aside so I could wipe my own eyes.

"My stubborn girl." He gave me a sad, indulgent smile. "Tracy, how could I ever deny you anything you wanted?"

"Well, I can think of one thing," I sniffled.

"You've still got a concussion. I mean, it's bad enough that we're going to go again," he sighed.

"We're going ag—not the point. That's not what you're denying me. I mean, not the thing I'm thinking of, anyway," I said.

He caught my hand… and put it over his heart. "This, perhaps?"

A lump formed in my throat and I couldn't get the words out, so I just nodded.

"Ah, sweetheart. What makes you think it hasn't already been yours for a while now? Clearly you have too many toys," he grinned.

My heart pounded against my ribcage. "I-it's not a toy."

"I'm glad you think that way," he said softly.

I sat up, inadvertently taking his cock deeper inside me and making us both give a little moan. "You'd better not be teasing me."

"I wouldn't tease about this," he replied, his tone and eyes completely sincere.

"Okay, good." I took his hand and pressed it over my chest. "Because this has been yours from about the time you said 'I'm listening.'"

Nate blinked at me. "In my office?"

"Yes."

"After that disastrous way I mistreated you?!" he went on.

I shrugged. "Most people don't take me seriously–certainly not anyone I ever dated, not my parents... My brother and some friends do, but that's been brief and chaotic to say the least, so..."

"You wouldn't call this 'brief and chaotic'?" he asked with a half-chuckle.

"Okay, fair. I don't know. I guess I just always remembered from when I was eighteen that you were a good person. You were the first person I thought of when my parents cut me loose–the *only* one. I mean, if you think about it, there are a hundred people in our circle I *could* have called on for help. Yet I only thought of you," I pointed out.

His throat worked in a hard swallow. "But Tracy, I completely betrayed that trust within the first five minutes of seeing you again."

"You didn't see me; you saw *her*, and I'm sorry about that—"

He pressed a finger to my lips. "Nothing about that situation was your fault. Don't ever think that."

"But—"

Nate pulled me down for a kiss. "I am the most lucky, unworthy bastard who ever walked the earth. I have told myself that every day since you walked back into my life."

I felt my cheeks heat up. "You're trying to sweet talk your way into my pants, Daddy."

He let out a bark of laughter. "I'm already in your pants," he said, rolling his hips.

"I-I guess it worked, then," I moaned, bracing my hands on his shoulders.

"Like a charm." He took my hips and began helping me ride him. His dick filled me to the brim every time he pulled me down on it, slamming himself home. I began to babble, then beg, with need.

"Lean down for daddy," he said and I did so. "Lower. I want to feel those titties against my chest."

I nodded, past coherent conversation. My sensitive nipples began rubbing against his chest, feeding me more pleasure.

I was panting when my body found nirvana again. Nate nipped and sucked the same spot on my neck as before while he came inside me. It made me shiver. I didn't have far to go, but I collapsed on him when we were finished.

Nate kissed my hair and wrapped me in his arms. "You know I'm still more than twice your age, right?"

"Uh-huh," I responded, unbothered. I tiredly rubbed my palm over his nipple.

"Mm. Sweetheart, if you do that, we're never getting out of bed," he warned me.

"You say that like it's a bad thing," I said around a yawn.

He laughed. "I think you might have been made for me."

"Me, too. Guess God just decided you'd need to wait a bit longer." I kissed his shoulder.

Nate caressed my cheek and I looked up. "Worth it," he said, his eyes filled with emotion.

I thought my heart might burst. "Even after getting kidnapped and mixed up with Owen, and having to see Lillian again, and… and shooting people, and…"

He kissed me. "I'm just glad you're not going through any of this alone. And, if you recall, Owen is *my* baggage, not yours. I'm sure he was going to get around to me eventually."

"Okay." I took his hand and twined our fingers together. "You know… I want you to know… it's really okay if we get… you know… married."

"Is that what you want, though?" he asked.

"Well, I mean…" I searched for the right words. "I didn't believe in it, really. But I've had such terrible examples…"

Nate sat up on his arms. "Tracy, I will never do to you what your mother has done to so many other men. I mean, we even know now she never stopped loving your father, she was just going around as some sort of Mata Hari, getting resources and information for Owen and William Masterson Sr."

"That was a… bit of a… surprise, that's for sure," I admitted, still feeling mental and emotional whiplash.

"I was surprised, too." He made a face. "Actually, it was a complete mindfuck for me, so I have no idea what it must have been like for you."

"'Mindfuck' is a good word for it," I said. I wrapped my arms around his neck and cuddled into him. "Do we mind that dinner's getting cold?"

"I don't," he replied, completely unbothered. "Do you?"

"Not a bit," I agreed.

His hand trailed down my back and over my ass to cup me intimately. "Round three?"

"Yes," I replied, feeling his dick harden against my thigh. "Round three would be nice."

21

I DO

Nate

I am a horny teenager. At fifty, this was not a stage I thought I'd ever be repeating in my life. Yet, as Tracy slept against me–her bleach-blonde, wavy hair tickling my chest and her delectable, perky breasts rubbing against me with every breath she took–I was pitching a tent under the sheets for the umpteenth time. I couldn't deny the truth. But–because I was a fifty-year-old man–I let her sleep. I'd completely worn her out, and by rights, at my age, I should have had a heart attack and died about halfway through our activities. Apparently there was a point to all the grueling workouts I put myself through.

Luckily, I'd gotten us both showered and changed the sheets before she passed out on me. The fact that, half an hour later, all I wanted to do was get everything dirty again, was a personal problem. My dick throbbed, telling me, with a gorgeous, sweet, caring, coura-geous woman laying on me, it really didn't have to be.

I stroked her hair and she wrinkled her nose, burrowing into me.

All's fair in love and war, drifted through my mind.

"Fuck me, why did I have to say that?" I sighed, leaning against the headboard. I scrubbed a hand over my newly-shaven face and looked down at her. "You shouldn't want forever with an old man like me." I wanted to erase that whole conversation where I'd selfishly allowed myself to want things I shouldn't touch.

"I just want you to know, you're kind of a pain in the ass," she mumbled against my skin.

I couldn't help myself–I laughed. "Oh, am I?"

"Yes. You're all hung up on this age thing all the time. It's just a number," she said, rolling onto her back and rubbing her eyes.

"It's a big number," I replied. I kissed her forehead. "Sorry for waking you up."

"You didn't go to sleep with me," she complained. "It was hard to sleep without you."

"I was right here!" I chuckled.

She snuggled into me. "But you weren't sleeping."

"How could you even tell?" I asked.

"Because of the way you breathe. You breathe differently when you're asleep. Your heartbeat's different, too." She caught sight of my erection making a tent-pole in the sheets. "Oh. You could have said you were having trouble."

"I thought you were sleeping," I laughed. I wrapped an arm around her, holding her to my side. "Still, in all seriousness, you should be saving yourself for someone more your age."

"Saving myself?! It's a little late for that!" She let out a hearty guffaw. "Weren't you *just* dick-deep in me for like the..." Her mouth moved silently.

A chuckle that was more like the bray of a donkey burst out of me. "Are you counting?"

Tracy bit her lip, clearly trying not to let out a laugh at my expense. "That was... a sound..."

"You *are* counting." I wrestled her underneath me while she let out a shriek of surprise, then laughter. "You shouldn't make fun of a poor little old man."

"Mhm. There is nothing poor or old about you," she said. I hissed as she ran her hand up my shaft. "Certainly not little."

"Point taken," I groaned as she started stroking my cock up and down under the sheets. "Though we really should talk about the fact that I'm old enough to be your f—"

"Daddy," she interrupted, her hand stilling on my dick.

I groaned, my hips bucking against her hand, encouraging her to start again. "What?"

"Look at me," she said, her hand resting at the base of my cock. If she'd told me to walk over broken glass right then, I would have done it, just for the slightest chance she might jerk me off some more. I looked into her eyes, which were stern and very serious.

"You're not my father," she told me. "And you're not an old man. Nothing about you is any less worthy than some guy my own age. Do you understand me?"

"But—"

She squeezed and I yelped.

"No 'buts'. I will be happy and proud to be your wife. As long as you're happy to have me, then there's nothing more we need to discuss other than how we're getting out of here," she said.

"Give a man a chance, woman!" I eased her hand off my cock. I could see the bruised uncertainty in her eyes and sighed. "Tracy, I have not wanted anything in this world with any great passion for years. After your mother…"

"Now this is about my mother?" she protested.

I tapped her nose. "Listen."

"Hey! I'm not a Shih Tzu—"

I tapped her nose again. "Listen to me. I was bored of everything already when I met your mother, but–somehow–she made me feel… exhilarated. I wanted to give her everything. It was only money to me."

"Hm. This had better be going somewhere better than it's starting," she grumbled.

"It is. I promise. I did figure it out, after a while, that Lillian is all flash and no substance. But I still didn't want to let her go because I didn't want to be back in that wasteland of boredom she'd saved me from. When she divorced me, I was bitter at her, yes, but mostly at myself. I couldn't believe I'd let myself be used that way—and as we know now, probably even more than what I thought. I lived in that bitterness and boredom for years." I took a deep breath. "Then you came along, and I took that bitterness out on you."

"You know I forgave you for that, right?" she said, touching my hand.

I shook my head. "It was unforgivable, and it would have been even if you weren't a virgin."

"Well, it must be forgivable, because I did it and now you're forgiven," she responded stubbornly.

"Tracy—"

"If you keep beating yourself up over a stupid mistake—that I agreed to, by the way—I'm going to twist it off," she warned me. Her expression was severe, her eyes flashing.

I burst out laughing again. "I'm sorry, I'm sorry," I said between chuckles. "Just... the look on your face..."

"I'm dead serious, you." She shook her finger at me. That pushed me right over the edge. Soon, I was laughing so hard I was wheezing and holding my sides.

"Nate." She scowled, crossing her arms over her chest. I fought to catch my breath, then leaned over and kissed her.

"What was that for?" she spluttered, her cheeks flushing.

"Because you're adorable. I know. I know you're serious and I can't tell you how much it means to me that you've forgiven me. But I also have to forgive myself," I explained.

She threw up her hands. "You are so frustrating!"

"Yes, I am," I agreed. "And now, I'm going to finish my story."

"Fine," she sighed.

Even though I was erect, I still pulled her into my lap, my dick folding up between her back and my belly. "Now... where was I..."

"About three or four inches from where you want to be?" she suggested sweetly.

I chuckled. "You're not wrong, but we'll get to that."

To her credit, she didn't start rubbing or teasing me, settling back against my chest and letting me speak.

"After what I did, I knew immediately that I had to help you out of whatever situation you were in. You came to me in good faith and I abused you and your trust. Even before the FBI showed up, I knew I was going to fix the situation. That gave me purpose. *You* gave me purpose for the first time in a very long time. I'm grateful for that, despite everything that's happened since." I kissed her shoulder.

"Well, I mean, Lillian got *'exhilarating,'*" she mumbled.

I snorted. "Surely you know you're better than that."

"Than… being a bit jealous of my mother?" she hazarded.

"No. Well, yes, that, too. Just because you have nothing to be jealous of," I said. "What I mean to say is you don't need to be exhilarating. You're so much more than that. Exhilarating passes. But you…" I didn't trust myself to continue. "Anyway, I think my friend here is going to shrivel up and fall off if he can't be inside you right this second—"

Tracy let me roll her underneath me, but put a hand on my chest to stop me from doing anything else. "He's going to have to wait."

"He's going to be very disappointed," I replied, my stomach twisting with unease.

"What am I to you?" she asked.

I swallowed. "Is this a trick question?"

"No, not a trick question, or a trap or anything like that. I just… I'd like to know," she said, biting her lip. "I mean, last night you said the 'love and war' thing meant something, but today you're all skittish and guilty and…"

I dropped my chin onto her shoulder with a heavy sigh. "Tracy, if I tell you those kinds of things–the things I'm thinking that you want to hear–I'd be taking away your opportunities—"

"If you bring up the age thing again, I'm going to scream," she admonished me.

"It's not a small deal. What if I don't want kids at my age? What if I get sick within the next ten or twenty years? You'd end up taking care of me during the best years of your life. What if we have nothing in common due to the generations we grew up in? You don't understand my jokes. I don't understand yours. You have so much of your life left…" I tried.

"So do you! Fifty isn't a hundred, for God's sake! If you don't want kids, then we won't have any. And what about getting sick? I could get hit by a car tomorrow and *you'd* have to take care of *me*. And about jokes–either of us grew up on the moon! There are things we will understand and things we won't, but every couple has that just based on education and interests. I might have a lot of life left ahead of me, but I'd like to spend as much of it as possible with you," she responded angrily. "Ugh… you're just… you're… you're such a…"

"Yes?" I asked. "What am I?"

"*A man!* You think you've got everything figured out and you just won't *listen!*" she shouted.

I tried very hard not to laugh. I tried, but all the warm fuzzies she'd just showered me with gave me a soft feeling in my heart and while she was frustrated, all I could feel was joy.

"Don't you even DARE laugh, Nathaniel Alton!" she said imperiously. Tears welled in her eyes.

I hugged her tightly. "Okay."

"Okay?" she replied. "What's okay?"

I thumbed her tears away. "You make me feel manly, that's true."

"Well, if you could feel a little less manly…" she grumbled, hunched into me.

"But I also feel weak and happy, and terrified, and safe. But most of all, loved. That's the best feeling of all," I said.

"Oh." She nodded. "That's a lot better than 'exhilarated'."

I chuckled. "Yes. A lot."

"So… you love me?" she asked shyly.

"I do." It was easier to say than I thought it would be, but it also felt as though it'd been trying to leap out of me for days.

"Well, that's good. Because I love you, too," she said.

My heart swelled, as well as other body parts. "What do you suppose we do about that?"

"I think that first, you screw my brains out. Then we talk about how many kids you want to have," she responded.

I leaned her forward so I could push my cock inside. We both let out a sigh of relief. "Will they all look like you?" I asked, beginning to thrust.

"Mhm. Possible," she gasped.

"Then let's have a thousand."

22

THE WAITING GAME

Tracy

I followed Nate while he prowled the property like a caged animal. The more of it he saw, the more quietly frustrated he became.

Two days in, we knew the name of every guard, but not their rotations. It was clear they switched up their schedules constantly and with no apparent pattern. That was frustrating.

The beach house was surrounded by a high wrought-iron fence. If that wasn't enough, it was electrified! That was frustrating.

Inside the house, there were locks similar to those at Owen's mansion that could be activated to lock us down at any time—in the house or even just one room. That was frustrating.

Marina and the guards watched us walk around with indulgent expressions on their faces. The pool boy actually laughed. "How's it going?" he snickered as we walked the fence by the pool. "Find a way out yet?"

I could tell from Nate's expression that if he'd been thirty years younger and still hot-headed, the pool boy would be missing some teeth.

"You try being locked up some time," I snapped, because I was thirty years younger and pissed off. The pool boy laughed again and went back to checking PH levels.

"Who *are* these people?!" I asked Nate, furious, when we got back to our room. "Who thinks it's okay to keep people trapped in a hamster cage? And not want to help?!"

"I believe they're called 'assholes,'" he replied without missing a beat. He began stripping off his polo shirt.

"Yes, sex is a great idea," I said eagerly, pulling off my own t-shirt.

"I was thinking the pool, actually," he replied, though his eyes fixed hungrily on my bra.

"Really?" I gave him a coy smile as I reached behind me to unsnap my bra. "The pool is what you're thinking about right now?" I let my bra slide down my arms and onto the floor.

He groaned. "You don't play fair."

"Who said I was playing, Daddy?" I grinned.

Nate walked over to me and palmed my naked breasts. "I was thinking… maybe we could… observe it all… while pretending to relax in the pool… but fuck me…" he murmured, peppering my face and neck with kisses.

"I'd like to, if you think the pool can wait," I teased, reaching between us and rubbing his dick through his shorts.

"Sweetheart, I'd put the second coming on hold to have you," he growled, massaging my breasts while nipping my shoulder.

I now had three hickeys on my neck that he was tending like his own personal garden. My shoulders seemed to be the next order of business. With a soft smile at his obsession, I unzipped his shorts and scooped his rigid cock out of his boxers.

He groaned.

"Bed?" I asked innocently.

"Yes. Bed," he managed. He backed me to the bed and then toppled me onto it. "Shorts."

I understood the order. While he shoved his down, I wriggled out of mine. "So, what were you hoping would happen in the pool that would make all the difference in your recognizance?" I asked, curious.

"Bikini," he grunted, thumbing my clit while he slid into me. I was wet and ready, anyway. I was all the time when it came to him.

I arched my back and moaned. "B-bikini?"

Nate nodded, beginning to thrust hard and fast, just the way we both wanted it. We could burn off some frustration and anger at our situation that way. "You. Bikini. Stunning."

"You think I can knock 'em dead with my boobs?" I laughed, then whimpered and dug my nails into his shoulders as he hit juuuuust the right spot.

"Hell yes." He framed my breasts with his hands. "These are exactly why men marched on Troy."

I swatted his arm. "So you think Helen was hanging her chest over the city wall saying 'dinner's on, come and get it'?"

"Absolutely." He grinned at me and squeezed my breasts, rubbing and pinching my nipples while he worked his cock in me.

Pretty soon, my eyes were rolling into the back of my head and I cried out, clawing his back. He groaned and came hot inside me. "Ahh, Tracy. Yes."

I clung to him, well-aware that this would only be the first of several rounds. It always was.

KNOCK KNOCK KNOCK

Except perhaps... today...

KNOCK KNOCK KNOCK!

"What?" Nate barked, carefully pulling out of me and tossing the comforter over my naked body.

"Hellloooo! Nate-y-boo!" my mother's voice filtered through the door.

I groaned.

Nate, who had yanked on his boxers and was halfway to the door, froze. He then proceeded to put the rest of his clothes on as well before answering. He opened the door just a crack, blocking Lillian's view of me. "What?"

"Oh, Nate-y-boo. You act like I haven't seen it all before," she trilled while trying to push the door open, but Nate didn't budge.

"Oh, it must be *sweetheart* who is en flagrante. All right, I understand. Meet us in the living room, won't you? There's a good boy."

"We'll be a minute," he replied stubbornly.

"I'll give you two." The male voice made my blood run cold.

"Owen?" I mumbled, clutching the comforter tighter.

Nate had also stiffened. "Owen."

"Morgan's here, too. We're having the loveliest reunion. Do come and join us," Lillian said.

"Two. Minutes," Owen repeated.

Nate unceremoniously slammed the door in their faces and locked it. The lock immediately slid back open. "Fuck."

I threw the comforter off and started hunting down my clothes. I wasn't going to be caught naked in two minutes! Nate bent down to help, holding my panties and shorts so I could step into them and doing up my bra behind my back. Just when I'd finished pulling my t-shirt down, the door beeped and swung open of its own accord.

"See? Just the right amount of time," Owen said, raising a martini glass.

Nate ground his teeth. "We're not some toys, Owen. You could have caught her naked."

"Oh, my dear Nathaniel: You *are* my toys–and I would have been tickled to see Tracy naked. Why should you be the only one who has that privilege?" His slimy smile made me feel oily all over.

Nate took a step toward him, towering over him and glaring. Lillian and Morgan both took out their guns.

Owen laughed. "You really have no sense of self-preservation. I mean, if you're dead, of course we'll marry her off to someone equally–if not more–advantageous. I'd take her myself, but I'm afraid she'd bite my dick off."

"Nate," I said, touching his back. "Please don't."

Nate's nostrils flared, but he took a step back and put an arm around me. "I'm her husband. That's why I'm the only one who has that privilege."

"Oh good! You've accepted, then. What happy news." Owen

clapped his hands as best as he could with a martini in one. He turned to me. "Are you pregnant yet, do you think?"

I stared at him. "Pardon?"

"Obviously you two aren't using protection, so I thought I'd ask," Owen said. "The only camera feed I seem to get from this place is you two copulating like bunnies, so I thought I'd ask."

"That's none of your business," Nate interjected, though he had paled a bit.

I wrapped my arm around his waist. "My IUD is good for another year."

Nate relaxed.

Owen looked sharply at my mother. "Care to explain, Lillian?"

"I didn't know she still had one!" Lillian responded defensively. "I mean, we had to do *something* just in case she had some youthful indiscretion…"

"Though that never happened, did it, Nathaniel?" Morgan chuckled.

"I'm not commenting on private matters. You've already crossed a line," Nate said, putting an arm around me. "If you came to talk about a wedding–yes, we are both on board with your plan. If that's all you came to talk about, if you don't mind, Tracy and I are going to go get a late lunch." He began steering me toward the staircase.

"That sounds like a lovely idea!" Owen stood and he, Lillian, and Morgan followed us down the stairs, through the living room, and into the kitchen.

Marina appeared out of nowhere, making me jump. "Shall I make some sandwiches, sir?" she asked Owen.

"That would be lovely, Marina. Let's take our repast in the living room, shall we?" Owen said pleasantly.

"That sounds wonderful," Lillian gushed. She and Morgan sat side-by-side on one of the loveseats, smiling and cooing at each other like two teenagers.

Nate escorted me to the other loveseat and draped an arm protectively around my shoulders as we sat down.

"I think it's adorable that you still think you could protect her from me," Owen chuckled.

"I think it's adorable that you still think you'd come out of an altercation like that alive," Nate said while I shuddered. "If I died, I'd take you with me at least."

Nate stared Owen down. Owen stared right back. The air became thick with tension.

"Oweeeen," Lillian simpered. "Stop. They won't know you don't mean it, and it will ruin lunch."

"Hm. I wouldn't want to ruin lunch." Owen smiled at my her. "You're right; of course, Lillian."

"She usually is," Morgan said with great devotion.

But Lillian was wrong. When Owen looked back at me, I could tell he meant it; his dark little heart had its sights set on using me to torture Nate.

Nate knew it, too. His arm tightened around me as Marina set a plate of assorted finger sandwiches between us.

Owen picked up a cucumber sandwich and casually began to munch on it. "So, wedding plans."

Lillian perked up instantly. "Yes! There's going to be a canopy on the beach, a local minister, and Tracy is going to wear the most gorgeous white sundress..." She chirped along happily about all the details of our spontaneous elopement. "Then, of course, a photo op when we have dinner with them in town–have to meet the parents, after all! It will be all over the media within hours."

"And have you planned the reception back in Minnesota?" Owen asked.

"Right down to the NDAs," Lillian smiled. "We can't have people knowing that the reception was planned before the elopement even happened."

"That is true." Owen took a sip of his martini. "Yes, this should shape up nicely."

"Why?" Nate suddenly asked.

"Why what?" Owen replied.

"Why make Tracy marry me? I won't lie and say I'm unhappy about it, but I'd like for you to make it make sense," Nate said.

Owen laughed. "That's easy. Everything was just fine, Nate, until you agreed to help our Tracy here. Then, you became some sort of crusader. I could kill you, but as you know, I'd rather toy with you for a while. But in order to toy with you, I need you on a short leash. I can't have you biting me. There is too much at stake for that. So, I thought since she'd already decided to hitch her wagon to yours, I'd give you Tracy, our other little crusader. You won't do anything stupid while it could affect her. And she won't do anything stupid when it could affect you. See? No fuss, no muss."

"And after you're done playing with me?" Nate asked, his arm tightening further.

"That could take *years*," Owen said.

"Oweeeeen," Lillian complained. "You said you'd make sure our baby was happy."

Owen frowned and my mother quickly stopped pouting. "Your daughter betrayed us. Every breath she takes from now on is a gift."

"Now, see here, Owen…" Morgan began.

"You two have one job: to do as I say. If I wanted your opinions, I'd ask for them," Owen snarled. "If following orders is too difficult for you, I can see a convenient car accident in your future. Now, do we have a problem?"

My parents shook their heads. "No, of course you're right, Owen," Dad said.

"I know I am." Owen swiveled his attention back to Nate and me. "Now, the wedding is tomorrow. Don't disappoint me, you two."

I swallowed the fear in my throat. "We won't."

2 3

ACTS OF DESPERATION

Nate

"You still want to try the bikini thing?" Tracy asked me, even while she pulled up the scant triangle that was the bikini bottoms.

"Yes," I replied, watching her shimmy it up her legs and silently congratulated myself for being the luckiest bastard who ever lived. "I want to see if I can see any holes in their security when they're distracted."

She looked out the window. "It's almost sunset."

"Our friends overstayed their welcome," I grumbled. "There's still enough time. We can't do it tomorrow because we're getting married."

"They'll be letting us out on the beach, then," she pointed out, sliding the bikini top up her arms. "Maybe they'll leave an opening there?"

I watched her fit the cups over her breasts and had to sternly tell my body to calm down. It didn't work, but I tried. Tracy bit her lip, trying not to laugh.

"It's not as funny as you think," I scolded her with a grin.

"It really is," she countered. With a look innocent as an angel's, she turned and presented her back to me. "Would you mind doing me... up?"

I snorted. "Minx."

"You know it," she agreed unrepentantly.

I went to her and tied the bikini behind her. Then I ran my fingertips down her bare spine, causing her to shiver.

She looked over her shoulder at me and I kissed her. "Mm. Daddy."

"You know it," I quipped. I wrapped my arms around her and pulled her back against my burgeoning erection.

Tracy doubled down and ground her ass against me.

"Fuck," I swore, dropping my forehead onto her shoulder. "Fuck. I wish we had time..."

"You don't think you're going out there like that, do you?" she asked, incredulous.

"I don't think I have much of a choice," I sighed. "Fuck."

"Well... what if I walk ahead of you and then we do it in the pool?" she suggested.

I stopped breathing. "With all those guards around?!"

"I mean, they're watching us on camera anyway, right?" she said.

She had a point. "I still don't like the idea," I growled.

"Possessive much?" she laughed. "No, I mean it. You wanted to see what would happen if they got distracted. Why don't we go all out?"

"Because it's bad enough I'm going to let them see you as nearly-naked as you are right now," I grunted. "That's already driving me insane."

"Pfft!" she giggled. "Like you *let* me do anything. You may be my daddy, Nate, but you're not my dad."

"Is it so wrong for a husband to not want other men ogling his wife?" I asked.

Tracy turned in my arms. The way that made her brush against my erection did not help the situation. "Nate, I want to help us get out of here. So that means if I have to show a little tit, I'm fine with it. They won't be able to see what's going on under the water. Please don't be jealous. We're a team. Let's see what we can accomplish together."

I didn't like it. I didn't like it one bit. But she was right. I couldn't stop her from doing it, and it just might help. "Just this once."

She smiled. "Glad you see things my way. Oh! We should probably do it on one of the chaise lounges so they get a really good view."

I scowled. "What happened to the pool idea? I prefer that idea—hot being able to see what we're doing underwater and all that."

"Yes, but it won't be as attention-grabbing," she said.

"No, but it will make me feel better," I argued.

Tracy placed a hand on my cheek. "We need to try everything, right? I only want to have to do this once. Go big or go home, right?"

The idea that I'd have to expose her to those men a second time made my stomach turn. "Fine."

"Good. Now let's get out there for the ogling," she said, stepping back and taking my hand.

I followed behind her, murder in my heart. Even though it had been mostly my idea, I did not want those men looking at her.

We walked out to the pool just as the sun was dipping toward the horizon. I started toward the water, making one last ditch effort to make the situation less painful. However, she grabbed my wrist in a stronger grip than I expected and dragged me to one of the chaise lounges around the edge of the kidney-shaped pool.

"Tracy, I really don't..." I tried as she pushed me back onto the lounge.

She got on top of me and silenced me with her lips.

I thought I might have lost my hard-on at the prospect of what we were about to do, but with her in my lap, my dick stayed perfectly erect.

"Can you see?" she asked, taking my hands and placing them on her breasts.

"See?" I echoed, my brain short-circuiting.

Tracy put her hands on my shoulders and ground against the front of my swim trunks. "The security and the guards and all that. That's why we're here, right?"

"Uh…" This was a challenge I'd completely missed when planning. How was I ever going to be able to concentrate while she was riding me?! I wasn't even inside her yet and I couldn't form a coherent thought. "Yes… that's why we're here…"

She gave me a wry smile. "I'm flattered that I've got this magical power over you where every time we touch, you turn into a mindless sex maniac–but you need to concentrate today."

"Mindless sex maniac," I agreed, massaging her breasts.

That made her giggle, then moan as I paid special attention to her nipples. "What am I saying? You make me a complete brainless puddle of goo. We're never going to pull this off!"

I took several deep breaths, then reluctantly slid my hands from her breasts and around her back. I pulled the tie on her bikini top. "Diving board."

"Hamster. What's with the random words?" she asked as I slid her top down her arms and tossed it onto the table next to us.

"You. Go diving. Then maybe hang out in the sun before it sets. Ham it up. Let them watch you," I said.

"Oh." She backed off my dick and got off me and the chaise. Tapping her chin, she replied, "That's not a bad idea."

"I know. That's why I hate it," I grouched.

Tracy smiled and leaned in to give me a long, slow kiss. "You watch the guards," she whispered against my lips. "I'll only be watching you."

My topless future wife then swayed her hips all the way over to the diving board.

I hoped and prayed the water was warm.

It wasn't.

She dove in and came up with a gasp and very pert nipples. Then she gave the most empty-headed giggle I'd ever heard in my life.

As predicted, the guards' attention turned to her. They stared like starved dogs presented with a steak and told to 'leave it.' I couldn't blame them. I'd seen the show and ridden all the rides—and intended to keep riding them until my last breath—and knew that it was all well worth the price of admission. Still, they were getting a taste of what should only be mine, and I hated it.

Other guards appeared. Apparently, word traveled fast.

Tracy's tits bounced as she skipped from the steps and around the other side of the pool to dive again. And again. And again.

At least twenty guards came, many abandoning their posts to watch the show.

If only there were someone on the outside who could take advantage of the situation; it wasn't as though I was stupid enough to try to take on twenty guards. Maybe in my younger years, and maybe if Tracy were in some direct sort of danger, but not now. Trying to go Chuck Norris on twenty guards would be the height of stupidity.

She giggled in the pool and did the backstroke. Beads of water trickled down her breasts and I knew the other men were counting every one.

I looked past the men to the gatehouse, still pretending to indulgently watch my young bride. They'd abandoned it in favor of satisfying their curiosity–I'd known they would. Seeing those perfect tits and ass covered by clothing was not nearly the same experience. In their position, I would have abandoned my post and shot myself in the leg to see half of what they were getting to see now.

I realized I'd finished my reconnaissance and was now just letting myself get more and more angry. *At this rate, I'm going to explode*, I reflected. "Tracy, sweetheart, let's go inside."

"But daddy…" she whined.

The guards' eyes bugged out.

I stood up and held out my hand. Tracy frowned at it in genuine confusion, clearly thinking I shouldn't be finished yet.

"Daddy wants to give you a present. Your favorite." I added a dirty grin for effect.

"O-okay, Daddy." She came over to me.

I grabbed a towel from a basket under the table and wrapped her in it. It was a big beach blanket towel, so it covered her from neck to toes. "Let's go practice for our wedding night."

"Whatever you want, Daddy," she responded in her empty-headed voice.

Once we were free, I was going to ask her to never use that voice again. It came in handy in this situation, and probably would in future situations, but it set my teeth on edge. Tracy was not an idiot and I liked that about her. It made me burn to think what sort of upbringing she'd had where she'd had to perfect such an act, where her intelligence wasn't valued, where—

"Daddy?" she asked as we stood, unmoving, on the cement. "Are we going inside?"

The guards were dispersing by now. I nodded and swept her up in my arms. "We're going inside, sweetheart." I carried her through the back double doors of the wisteria-covered house and toward the staircase.

Marina was waiting there. "Pardon the intrusion, sir, but Mrs. Franz was hoping you could try on your wedding clothes before tomorrow."

I looked down at Tracy, who shrugged. "That's news to us."

"Mrs. Franz didn't want you destroying them. I'm to supervise," Marina explained.

"We're not going to destroy them," I sighed. "What, does she think we want to go down to the beach naked?"

"Be that as it may, I'm to take Miss Franz…" Marina began.

I laughed. "You're not taking Miss Franz anywhere."

"But, sir—"

"If you need to do some sort of fitting this evening, you're doing it in front of me," I said in my don't-you-dare-fuck-with-me tone.

"Then you'll see the bride in her dress before the wedding, sir," Marina argued.

I set Tracy on her feet and put an arm around her. "What do you think, Tracy?"

"I think I'd rather you see me in my dress than risk being separated," she replied, pressing into my side.

Marina's lips thinned. "They said you'd be difficult."

"They were right," I concurred.

Then, Marina pulled out a gun.

"For the love of fuck…" I murmured, my brain calculating how to disarm her. I tensed, ready to rush her.

Two guards with guns appeared from either hallway. "Don't do it, Sarge."

Marina pointed her gun at Tracy's forehead. "Back off, Mr. Alton."

Shaking with rage, I took a step back, my heart tearing to shreds at the frightened little squeak Tracy gave when we were no longer touching. I was so damn tired of feeling so *fucking* helpless!

One guard grabbed my arms and forced me to my knees. The other kept a gun to my head.

"Nice trick with Tracy going topless. I never thought you'd let her," Marina said as she put a hand on Tracy's shoulder. "Upstairs! You—up!"

Tracy gave me a desperate look, and something inside me snapped.

24

HERE COMES THE BRIDE

Tracy

A gun went off.

I expected to feel some sort of pain, or burning, or whatever a gunshot was supposed to feel like. Instead I felt… nothing.

"Get behind me," Marina said, quickly shoving me between her back and the staircase. "Sir, that is not acceptable behavior!"

It was then that I realized that: one–I hadn't been shot, and two–Nate was going ballistic.

I looked over her shoulder and saw one guard writhing on the floor while Nate, in a blur of motion, disarmed the other one. The guard raised his arms. Nate didn't even hesitate. He shot him in both kneecaps.

"Mr. Alton!" Marina snapped. She touched her ear. "Ugh. Watchtower, this is Merry Maid. Sergeant has gone rogue. Repeat, Sergeant has gone rogue. Request backup."

As the two guards laid on the floor groaning, Nate pointed his gun at Marina. "Get us out of here."

"No," she responded, perfectly calm. "I assure you, whatever you could bring yourself to do to me if I don't take you out of here will be one-tenth as bad as what Mr. Jorgensen will do to me if I do."

His eyes flicked to mine. "Go upstairs, Tracy. Barricade yourself in our room."

"But I want to go with you," I protested.

"Do it," he ordered, his tone brooking the argument. It was actually kind of scary.

I was about to argue with him anyway, but the doors burst open and ten guards flooded in from all directions.

"Go!" Nate barked. Terrified, I did as he said, sprinting upstairs in my towel and down the hall to our room. Marina was hot on my tail until we reached the top of the stairs. There was another gunshot and she shrieked, hitting the floor with a moan of pain.

As soon as I was in our room, I slammed the door shut. I tossed off my towel and began dragging any piece of furniture I could move in front of the door.

I could hear the scuffle downstairs. My heart pounded with worry. Would Nate be okay? They couldn't kill him, right? *Right?!*

Nerves fraying, I sat down on the bed, which had been too heavy to move. For the first time, I noted my wedding dress laid out on it. A beautiful, simple white sundress, as my mother had described.

As the yelling and bashing sounds continued downstairs, I wondered if I was going to have occasion to wear it.

I gently hugged the dress to myself and choked back a sob.

Nate, please be okay.

I HADN'T EVEN REALIZED I'D FALLEN ASLEEP, HOLDING MY WEDDING dress like an emotional support blanket. I also wasn't sure what had woken me up.

But then, there it was again. "Daaaaahling! Yoo-hoo!" Lillian called through the barricaded door.

I glanced through the curtains. It was just barely dawn. Definitely a time of day I'd never thought my mother had seen. "Where's Nate?" I rasped, then cleared my throat. "Where's Nate?"

"Oh, he's fine, darling. He was just feeling his oats, as they say," she chirped. "It's time for you to get ready for your wedding! Clear that junk away and open the door. The hair and make-up people are here and you need to shower."

"I'm not doing anything until I see Nate," I replied stubbornly.

My mother sighed. Then my father chimed in. "Tracy, this is your father speaking. You listen to your mother. We've all got a long day ahead of us—"

"Nate. Now," I insisted, not moving an inch.

"When did you become so obstinate? I swear," Morgan grumbled. Soon, he began a one-sided conversation. I could only assume he was on the phone. "Owen? Yes. She's being stubborn. She won't do anything we say unless she sees *him*. Uh-huh. Yes. You're right, it was to be expected. Can they bring him up? Uh-huh. Yes, I under-stand. We'll try. Otherwise, we're going to need to get some strap-ping young men up here to get through that door. I'll keep you posted."

I waited to hear what my father had to say.

"Tracy, he won't be able to see you until the wedding. He's a little banged up and they're working on making him presentable," he said. "You're just going to have to open the door and get ready for the day, or we're going to call in some guards to shove their way in, and I'm not sure you'd like that."

I hugged my wedding dress, noting that without the towel, all I had on were my bikini bottoms from the night before. "I'm going to shower and get dressed."

"You're going to open this door first," Dad rumbled.

"I'm not… dressed for company," I said.

"Then put on a robe. Your mother wants to see you," he responded, not giving an inch.

With a sigh, I put my dress down, flattening it carefully on the bed. Then I went to the closet and pulled out one of Nate's t-shirts. It covered me from neck to mid-thigh. I decided that was good enough. Even though he'd never worn this shirt, it made me feel closer to him, and that offered some comfort.

"Tracy?" Morgan said imperiously.

Without answering, I started shuffling furniture away from the door.

"Oh good. I knew you'd see reason." He went quiet after that.

I dreaded the fact that he and my mother were waiting on the other side of the door. When I cleared the area and opened the door, my parents smiled at me. It was creepy. "I'm just going to shower and get dressed, okay? See? I'm fine."

"Aw, she's wearing one of his shirts. That's so sweet," Lillian cooed.

"I knew we made the right decision," Morgan added, kissing my mother's temple.

That set me off. "You... decision? What kind of decision do you think *you're* making? Don't kid yourselves. It's Owen's decision."

Lillian's expression soured. "You don't need to be a brat about it."

"Yes, you're upsetting your mother," Morgan said, frowning at me.

I laughed, sounding a bit hysterical even in my own ears. "Oh, yes, I see. My biggest concern right now is that I'm upsetting my mother. My bad. You'd think I wasn't being held hostage and forced into a marriage that you all want but never asked us about. And this is all to cover up an international crime ring that exploits children and prophets off of war. No, really, don't mind me. I'm a bad daughter. That's what we should all really be worried about."

"Tracy, go shower," Dad snapped.

"Gladly!" I replied, slamming the door in their faces.

I locked the door behind me, but I knew it wouldn't be any great barrier. And I was right. As I stood under the shower spray, angrily shampooing my hair, I heard a light rapping on the wall.

"Tracy, darling," my mother said.

I could see well enough through the frosted glass to watch her take a seat at the large vanity. "What?" I asked testily.

"It's really not as bad as you think. You'll be well provided for and start out with a man you really quite like a lot," she cajoled. "Just—"

I turned off the water and slammed back the door, making it shake in its track. "'Start out'? What do you mean, 'start out'?"

"Well, I mean, of course once Owen is finished with Nate-y-boo —"

"Don't call him that," I seethed.

She winced. "Fine. Sorry. Old habits."

"What do you think is going to happen when Owen finishes with Nate?" I demanded.

"He'll be dead, of course." She made it sound normal, like the natural order of things.

My stomach clenched. "I don't like that plan."

"I know, darling, but you'll get used to it." She reached out to pat my hand.

I snatched it away. "And I suppose after Nate, I'm supposed to marry and exploit some other advantageous billionaire for the cause. Whore it around like you?"

Lillian was on me in seconds–she slapped me hard. "Don't say things like that about your mother!"

I touched my cheek. "When were you ever my mother?"

She trembled with rage. "Finish your shower. I'll be out in the bedroom. We've got to get you ready, and I need to tell the make-up artist that now we're going to need more concealer." She whirled around and stalked out of the bathroom.

My cheek throbbed, but more importantly, my chest was tight with panic. Was this really the future they had laid out for me? Was Nate really going to be killed? How soon? Was there any way for us to prevent it?

Thoughts ran round and round in my mind until the water ran cold.

"Tracy Ann Franz! Finish your shower and get out here now!" Lillian shouted from the bedroom.

Nate will know what to do, I decided. *We'll get through this together.* I conditioned my hair, then stepped out of the shower and wrapped my hair up in a towel after drying off. I took my sweet time; I was in no mood to oblige my mother.

"Finally!" she said when I walked out of the bathroom. There were four women I didn't recognize standing in the room with her. "These are your stylist and make-up artist, and their assistants. You've kept us all waiting, and they're not cheap."

"Okay," I replied absently. I decided it wasn't worth engaging with her anymore. She was completely on the enemy's side and didn't give a damn about me.

Her eyes narrowed. "Put on this robe, then go sit at the vanity."

"So, back in the bathroom," I needled her as I took the robe and put it on.

"Yes," she responded tightly. "Back in the bathroom."

I turned on my heel and marched back into the bathroom. The stylist, make-up artist, and their assistants followed me.

In a matter of hours, they turned me into a perfect little doll. No sign of my mother's marks, or even Nate's, showed on my skin. They'd even styled my hair so my stitches weren't visible.

"Perfect," my mother gushed when they were finished. "Now we just have to get you in your dress without ruining anything. Speaking of which, you should not have squashed it like you did last night. I was afraid we might not get the wrinkles out!"

"Yes, Mother," I gave another noncommittal response.

She pursed her lips. "You are on my last nerve, Tracy."

"Yes, Mother," I said again.

Her breath hissed out slowly. "Ladies, get the dress on her. I'll find the sandals."

The women helped me step into the sleeveless sundress, then gently pulled and tugged on the fabric until it was perfect.

Mother snatched a pair of white flat sandals that matched the dress out of the closet and tossed them on the floor in front of me. "Put them on."

"Yes, M—"

"STOP IT!" she snarled.

I considered saying it again anyway, but I was tired of our war. She didn't mean enough to me to annoy–not anymore. I stood silently instead.

"Oh for God's sake say something!" Lillian yelled.

"Where is Nate?" I replied.

"On the beach, as long as all's gone to plan," she said.

"Then let's go to the beach." I pushed past her and the other women and headed out into the hall.

"You are such an ungrateful brat," she muttered, catching up to me. "After all your father and I have done for you…"

"What? Groomed me to be the village bicycle for billionaires?" I muttered, forgetting my promise to myself not to engage with her.

Lillian grabbed my arm. "Stop being a bitch!"

"Start being a mother! If you're even capable of that!" I shouted back.

"Now, now, ladies. It's Tracy's wedding day. I'd think we'd all be a bit happier," Owen said from the bottom of the stairs. He was wearing a beige linen suit with a lily in the lapel.

"She's impossible," Lillian complained.

"She won't always be," he responded smoothly. He offered me his arm while looking me up and down appreciatively.

I wanted to claw his eyes out. "No, thank you."

"So polite," he chuckled. "I'm afraid you don't have a choice, unless you want to marry me instead of Nate."

I took his arm faster than I'd ever done anything in my entire life.

"There we go. Well, off to the beach. Morgan is already down there. I'm sure we're all excited to get the festivities underway." He gallantly escorted me through the back door of the beach house and through the now-open back gate, down to the beach.

I didn't see Nate anywhere. "What's going on?" I asked.

"Oh, I'm sorry, you must have misunderstood," Owen said while my mother sat down in a white, wooden, collapsible chair next to my father.

"What do you mean, misunderstood?" I asked.

"You *are* marrying me."

25

LOST

McKenzie

"Will's going to be okay, honey," my mother said for the thousandth time in two weeks. "He's just in jail. He can't get hurt there."

Dad winced when I looked up from my cot. It was true, I probably looked like crap warmed over. He stroked my hair, exchanging a worried glance with my mother. "They'll feed him and take care of him. Once this is all over, they'll let him go. Then we'll all be together again."

"Prison is just an easy place for them to get him. You know it. I know it. Let's not pretend, okay? I know you mean well, and I love you, but this is very, very bad," I whispered. I felt so empty inside. A part of me was missing, and I didn't know how to get him back.

"Oh, it's not as bad as all th—" Mom tried.

"Jacey, I think it's best if you don't lie to your daughter, if you'll forgive me," Garrett said, poking his head into our tent.

Right. Tents weren't exactly soundproof.

"It's not a lie!" Mom protested. "He's in federal custody. What could possibly happen?"

Even my dad gave her an incredulous look.

Mom swallowed. "Is it bad?"

"It's very bad," Garrett replied. "If they want him dead, it would be very easy to kill him there."

"Oh." She was quiet while bile rose in my throat.

Will...

"Still, he's safer there than some of the other places we've been," she tried to reason.

"That's... not saying a whole lot, love," Dad said.

"No... but..." She looked troubled. "He's practically our son, Caleb." She turned to Garrett. "Isn't there something we can do? I mean, do you have access to Will's money and there would be someone we could bribe or hire...?"

Garrett sighed. "Even if I did have access—and I don't—his accounts would be frozen by now. And I don't know anyone who could break Will out of federal prison."

"Oh." I could see my mom's brain was working overtime to come up with a solution.

"Why don't we let McKenzie rest some more," Dad said softly to her, taking her shoulders and turning her gently toward the other side of the double tent. "That would be okay, right Garrett? We're not going anywhere today?"

"No. We're not." Garrett looked at me. "Will's going to need you to be more fighting fit so you can survive this. He'd be really concerned at how skinny you've gotten."

I snorted. "He's going to die in federal prison, right? So what's the point?"

"McKenzie!" Mom gasped. "No, don't say that!"

Tears pricked my eyes, then overflowed for the third time that day. "I don't want to live without him," I whispered.

"Fuck," Dad swore.

Garrett pushed past the tent flap completely and elbowed my parents aside. He knelt next to my cot with a stern look on his face. "Don't get suicidal on me. Next thing you know, your parents decide to join you and we're stuck with an empty tent and a whole lot of explaining to do."

"To who? Will? After they get him in prison?" I snorted.

He didn't respond, which made me suspicious. "You are working for Will, right?"

Dad tensed and pushed Mom behind him as we waited for his answer.

"I did," Garrett finally said. "But we needed someone to finance our continued escape. Mouths to feed and all that."

"Who's backing us?" Dad asked.

"You wouldn't believe me if I told you," Garrett responded. "Look, just think of him as a silent partner. He doesn't know where we are. He just sends money."

"What does he expect in return?" Dad demanded.

Garrett shrugged. "Just updates that you're okay. Which, clearly, you're not, McKenzie. I don't know about maybe getting you into some sort of facility for your mental health, but then, you'd be a sitting duck, too. We'd need a fake ID…"

"That doesn't answer my question," Dad said, still standing protectively in front of Mom. "I want to know what he *wants*."

"He wants McKenzie and Will to make it out okay on the other side of this thing. You two are just a bonus," Garrett sighed. "Really, I wouldn't be looking a gift horse in the mouth. I vetted him, okay? He's good people. At least as good as they come in his business."

"What's his business?" Dad kept grilling him.

"Um…" Garrett rubbed the back of his neck. "Targets and acquisitions."

Dad frowned. "'Targets and acquisitions'?"

"He's a mercenary, Dad," I said tiredly.

"He's a… you're taking money from a *hitman*?!" Dad bellowed. "How the *fuck* does that make sense?!"

"Food. Shelter," Garrett reminded him. "Transportation."

"How did you even… where… when… who the fuck is this person?! No, you know what? We're taking the Escalade and we're leaving you, Eric, and Dan. I knew there was something fishy going on, I just knew it!" Dad took my pillow from under my head. "McKenzie, get up. We're getting out of here."

I'm not sure what the expression on my face was, but it made my father's eyes darken with concern. "Why? What does it matter? We'll just fall into someone else's hands tomorrow."

"Caleb, in the first place, I have the keys," Garrett said with a long-suffering sigh. "Second, what are you going to do when you run out of gas? Where are you even going to go? You're not thinking this through."

"Garrett, my daughter is sick..." Dad responded, his voice cracking so slightly on the last word.

Garrett reached out and put a hand on his shoulder. "I know. And we're gonna fix that."

"I just don't think I can handle being bounced around between bad guys again," Mom spoke up. "At least Will's sister, Tracy, is safe with her father. Overseas by now, I would expect."

Garrett winced.

"You've had news?" I asked, sitting up on my elbows.

"It's... not good news. I was hoping I wouldn't have to tell you. Especially with how sick—"

"Out with it," Dad said.

Mom cleared her throat.

"Please," he added with a grunt.

"Tracy's been taken by the Masterson organization, along with billionaire Nathaniel Alton, who she'd enlisted for help," Garrett told us reluctantly. "They've basically disappeared."

"They disappeared... a billionaire?" I gaped. "I mean, don't they basically just get billionaires to sign up?"

"By all accounts, Alton is too moral for that. But I suppose anything's possible if you wear a person down with time," Garrett said.

I shook my head. "Fine. Okay. So we're all fucked—"

"McKenzie! Don't use that language," Mom admonished me.

"Fine. We're all screwed. But you say we've got a mercenary sugar daddy right now. I want to meet him," I said.

Garrett's eyes narrowed with suspicion. "Why?"

"I want to look him in the face when I ask him what it would take to get Will, Tracy, and Mr. Alton out of their situations," I replied. "He can have whatever he wants that I can give him."

"No," Dad interrupted. "He can have whatever he wants that *I* can give him."

"We," Mom corrected him.

Garrett wiped a hand over his face. "I don't think it's advisable to have you three out in the open, and he won't come here in case he's followed."

"We have to shower anyway. I don't want another bath in the lake," Mom said. "I mean, I'll happily do it if I have to, but if we're finally leaving the woods… why not a suite at some mid-level hotel chain? I know it might be cramped, but you three can take one room with a trundle and we'll take the other. We'd only stay one night, and he could meet us in the lounge."

"I don't know…" Garrett murmured, but I could tell we were wearing him down.

"And laundry." I dangled the bait. I knew how much he hated doing laundry in the lake.

Garrett groaned. "You don't play fair. All right, will it keep you from trying to kill yourself for the time being?"

I made a cross-my-heart sign. "As long as there's some hope that he can help, I'll stick around."

"Fine," he muttered. "Start packing up. We'll leave within half an hour."

Victorious, I rolled off the cot as he left. I began packing my things and collapsing my cot.

My parents watched me, looking concerned.

"What?" I asked.

"You really have gotten quite a bit thinner," Mom whispered. "And in just two weeks!"

"I'll be fine," I insisted. "Now, let's go talk to a mercenary."

My parents looked at each other, then gave in with a sigh and went to pack their things.

Several hours, a shower, and many loads of laundry later, my parents and I sat casually surrounded by Garrett, Eric, and Dan in the hotel lounge, waiting for our mercenary benefactor to arrive. As the time slid slowly toward seven o'clock, an hour past when we were supposed to meet, I began to wonder if he was coming at all.

"He may have had a tail and decided it was too dangerous," Garrett suggested from the table next to ours. "He's very cautious. He's spent a long time in the industry without getting killed, so it's served him well, as he says."

I nodded, but felt a knot of disappointment in my stomach. I'd really wanted to begin negotiations with him today. It was good news to hear he'd been in the life a long time. He'd have a lot of connections, then.

Then I heard a soft thump-thump approaching the entrance to the lounge, getting louder the closer they got.

"That's him," Garrett confirmed as a man with a cane and a pronounced limp slowly made his way toward our table.

My parents rose to greet him.

I was too gobsmacked to leave my chair.

"HOOT?!"

ALSO BY M. FRANCIS HASTINGS

Once Bitten

Submitting to My Stepbrother series

Stranded With My Stepbrother

Snatched With My Stepbrother

Sequestered With My Stepbrother

Subpoenaed With My Stepbrother

Flirting With the Forbidden

Fleeing With the Forbidden

Fighting for the Forbidden

Forever With the Forbidden

Bound by the Betrayed

The Beguiling Baronets series

Deceiving the Duke

Dream Mates

Dream Weaver

Dream Reader

www.ingramcontent.com/pod-product-compliance
Lightning Source LLC
Chambersburg PA
CBHW070858160726
48004CB00003B/1138